BDSM Sex Stories

Hot And Wet Erotica Collection:
Taboo Sex Stories

By

Lana Grey

Respective authors own all copyrights not held by the publisher.

The information herein is offered for informational purposes solely, and is universal as so. The presentation of the information is without contract or any type of guarantee assurance.

The trademarks that are used are without any consent, and the publication of the trademark is without permission or backing by the trademark owner. All trademarks and brands within this book are for clarifying purposes only and are the owned by the owners themselves, not affiliated with this document

CONTENTS

01

Woman With A Plastic Face

His name was Liam. He had everything. He had a great job and had a girlfriend he loved more than anything. He earned a lot of money because of his job and he was very rich because of it. Also, he came from a rich family. Not extremely rich but he had everything he ever wanted since his childhood. So, pain and suffering was something unfamiliar for Liam because his parents made sure of that.

He became a software engineer and after a while, he started his own startup company. Then he managed to take his company to a global scale in a few years. Now, it's a multi-million-dollar company. He fell in love with Ava, only after he became a millionaire. He knew Ava since high school but he only became bold enough to ask her out after he became so rich. She said yes and they were inseparable after that.

Liam was not a good-looking guy, yet he couldn't be considered as ugly. But he had a typical look that nerds had. He looked a lot like Mark Zuckerberg, the creator of Facebook. He even spoke like him. On the other hand, Ava was the prom queen and she was beautiful in every way. Every man wanted her, and every woman wanted to be her. She was not just beautiful, but she had this classy look that made everyone love her. She had blonde hair that fell to her waist that was extremely straight. It always shined brightly like a diamond. Everyone would be amazed when they saw her hair. She always got offers to be on shampoo advertisements a lot just because of her hair. It was flawless. She had a face just as flawless as her hair. She always had this natural gold color tan. Some people said that she is the reason for Liam's wealth since her skin represents gold and prosperity. But Liam knew that he got his wealth before he became involved with her.

She had slanted eyes like a Chinese. She said that her grandfather from her mother side was from China. But her eyes were the only body parts that looked Chinese. So, her eyes gave a stunning beauty to her face with her skin color. She was five foot and six inches tall and when she wore heels, she looked like a goddess. Her body was second to none. She had breasts that were the size of coconuts and they were shaped like lemons. Her cleavage could hypnotize anyone in seconds. She had a flat stomach but also had a smooth six pack on it. The sides of her stomach also had muscles that showed. This is because she played tennis a lot. She was a pro tennis player.

She had relatively long legs, so everyone who had leg fetishes would go crazy for her, which was almost every man because there is no man on earth who doesn't love long and pretty legs. She always wanted to show her thighs when she dressed up. Even when she wore long dresses, she chose a dress with a split so she could show her entire leg. Her ass was also extraordinary. It was not so big, but her butt was the perfect size and shape. She always wore dresses to highlight the shape of her ass because she liked it when people admired her. She liked the attention that it brought her. She always wanted to be the spotlight of any event.

When she was in high school, she went out with lots of boys. She went out with bullies and most of the members of the school football team. It was like, even though she was the prettiest girl in the school, anyone could tap that ass if they are popular enough around the school. So, she was popular as a beautiful slut. But no one would dare to call her that to her face because they wouldn't want to ruin their chance of getting to sleep with her. Girls in her high school also wanted to be friends with her because she was considered a cool girl. Since every guy wanted to sleep with her, it was easy for other girls to get guys if they were with Ava. She had this "bitch attitude" throughout the whole time in high school because she was always with girls who wanted to use her to get laid.

On the other hand, the high school experience for Liam was the exact opposite. He was a complete nerd. Puberty hit him so hard and he had to wear braces on his mouth throughout the years in high school. His face was covered with pimples, so no one would even look at him. Therefore, he had no chance of getting Ava when he was in high school. She would never even notice him. He knew that but he loved her with everything he had anyway. Because of that, he wouldn't go out with any other girl. He became obsessed with her. That was one of the main motivations for him to become successful and rich because he knew that he would have a chance with her. So, when he finally got her, he felt like a god. He knew that he had everything, and he was finally satisfied with his life. After that, he was having a peaceful life with her.

He dated Ava for about a year and a half. Then he finally built up the courage to propose to her. She said yes. It was the happiest day of his life. He even bought her a house after that. He wanted Ava to have everything. Then he managed to marry her after a couple of months. It was a simple but very expensive and beautiful wedding. After that, they went on a month-long honeymoon around the world. Liam wanted to spend money as much as he could for Ava because he knew deep down that Ava loved him for his money. He was fine with it because after all, he thought that he could buy anything with money including happiness. So, for Liam, Ava was his happiness which he finally managed to buy. But he had one weakness, and that was that he trusted Ava too much because even though he knew that she was with him for his money, he thought that she loved him at least for that.

He was happily married to Ava for about a year. But then, he found out that she was not in love with him any at all. He caught her red-handed when she was cheating on him with her tennis instructor. She was just a gold digger after all. This broke Liam's heart to the core because Ava was the only woman he has ever been with. He had lots of chances to cheat on her because he was a millionaire, but he never did that because he loved her that much. Also, he had never slept with another woman before he was with Ava because he was in love with her long before he got a chance to be with her. So, this was more than he could handle. He had to file for a divorce but since Ava didn't sign a prenup, he had to give her half of his assets from his company and a lot of money. He didn't do anything to hurt her after that because deep down, he still loved her. But also, he grew a lot of hatred towards womankind at the same time because of what she did to him. He believed that she destroyed him, and she didn't deserve anything he gave her. But after everything, she managed to get half of what Liam owned.

This mentally broke Liam. His close friends tried to get him back on track by getting him laid a lot. He tried to sleep with women as much as he could but at first, he was not able to do any sexual activities with any women because he still loved Ava with all his heart. But after a while, he managed to get an erection without thinking of Ava and finally he managed to sleep with other women without crying like a kid. But he was never satisfied with it. The reason for that was, before his divorce, he had never experienced one-night stands. He loved only one woman and he only had sex with that one woman. So, it felt like something was missing for him in his latest sexual activities.

Liam usually was a very secretive person, especially with his feelings. That's why it took him years to build up the courage to talk to Ava. He could have easily got her a year earlier if he tried and that would have changed the whole outcome of how it turned out in the end.

Since he was rich, he managed to procure the services of a famous and superb therapist named Dr. Benjamin. His therapist got him to talk about his sexual feelings. Liam said to Dr. Benjamin, "I have lots of sex, doctor. But there is no satisfaction in the end. I mean I enjoy the sex and all and I cum all the time but that was it. There are no feelings afterward. I feel like there is some piece missing. And I can't figure out what that is exactly."

Dr. Benjamin responded, "Maybe it's because of your ex-wife. You still have feelings for her, and you are still trying to move on from that, so it's normal for you to feel like there is a part of you missing. It will fade away with time. But you have to have hope in order to achieve that peace. Otherwise, you will dwell in your past for the rest of your life."

"It's not that doctor. I know I still miss her. I know I still love her. I know that love will never fade away. But finally, I was able to accept the fact that she never had truly loved me. It's not that. It's something else. I just can't put my finger on it."

"Maybe you have hatred toward her. It's not that hard to hate something that you love so much. Maybe you feel hate toward Ava because of what she did to you. You felt abandoned after that. Maybe that's why you feel this way. She hurt you to your core, but you couldn't do anything to hurt her back. In return she managed to get most of your money. So, you might feel that she cheated on you more than with just sex. Maybe you feel like she cheated on you with your life. Maybe deep down, you believe that she doesn't deserve to be happy after what she did to you."

"Of course, I believe that. I mean believe me, I hate her more than anything, but how could the hatred I have towards her make me feel like there's something empty inside of me? I mean if that's the case, then I should feel angry, right?"

"Well, if that's the case, what you need is a way to express your anger. You can't just keep that much anger inside yourself and be like nothing is wrong. It's unhealthy. You must find a way to express that anger or find some way to get that anger out of your mind. Have you ever tried boxing?"

Liam said no to that. Then the doctor recommended him some boxing lessons so he could let some steam out through boxing.

After a couple of days, Liam had some boxing lessons with a good friend of his. He also was a good boxing coach. After some warm-ups, Liam had to go into the ring with another amateur boxer. His coach said to Liam to punch his opponent as hard as he could, but he wasn't able to do that because Liam was not much of a fighter and violence was something he was unfamiliar with his entire life. Then his opponent punched him with a light upper-cut and that was more than enough to knock Liam out cold. Liam realized that boxing was not an option and he didn't try that again.

So, the next week, he told his therapist what happened to him in the ring and said that boxing is out of the equation.

Then Dr. Benjamin said, "Well, I don't have more suggestions for you, Liam. But what I can say is, you must find a way to express your anger. Otherwise, it will eat you up from the inside. And it will only get worse. So, I suggest you find a way to remove that anger within yourself as soon as possible."

When he went home, he tried to think of a way to express his anger. He knew that he was not a violent man. He could never hurt a fly. So, it was something impossible for him. He tried to listen to black metal music and started to watch hard-core porn, but it was not satisfying for him. Then he called his best friend Mike. He knew Mike for a long time and he really trusted Mike with anything. Mike had a leadership position at another high profiled company. So, he was rich, and he always lived a playboy lifestyle. He was about as Liam's age and they were really good friends.

After Liam explained to Mike his situation, his friend said, "Don't worry bro. I got you. Meet me at my house Friday evening."

It's all he said to Liam. He asked Mike about what he had in mind, but he refused to tell him anything more than that. So, he couldn't wait to meet him on Friday. It was all he could think of. He knew that Mike would never disappoint him, and he really wanted to get rid of that emptiness out of his system. Then he went to Mike's house right on time. It was actually more like a mansion. It was bigger than Liam's house. Liam had a way bigger mansion when he married Ava but after the divorce, he had to give it to Ava. So, he bought a normal size house after that because he lived there alone by himself most of the time.

Greeting Liam at the door, Mike said, "Are you ready buddy? I'm gonna blow your mind."

Liam smiled and said, "Don't do that literally," then both of them laughed.

They went somewhere far away in Mike's car. At first, Liam asked if he could follow Mike in his car but Mike refused. He said that if they see an unfamiliar car, they will not let them in. Then they drove for about 45 minutes. Liam asked about where they were going but Mike refused to tell him anything. Instead, he just said, "Hang on buddy. You are in for a treat. Just trust me on this okay." Finally, they came to the place. It looked like an abandoned warehouse, but it was covered in a wall around it and there was only one gate. Mike stopped his car near the gate and honked a couple of times to a rhythm. Then the gate opened, and he looked at Liam and said, "That's the password here today. Pretty cool right?" Mike winked and drove his car inside.

It was a lot of security for an abandoned warehouse. Liam couldn't figure out why there was so much security and why the fuck they went there. Mike drove his car inside the warehouse and told Liam to get out of it. A big fat black man came and greeted Mike. He was wearing a lot of gold. He had more than 10 huge gold rings on his fingers and he had a huge thick gold chain around his neck. He was wearing a lot of gold earrings and had four gold teeth. There were a lot of diamonds on his gold rings and chain. He also had a couple of gold bracelets around his hand. More than half of him was covered in gold and it was so obvious that he was a gangster because he had a gold pistol on his waist, and he was not trying to hide it at all.

The man said to Mike, "Damn dawg. I haven't seen you here in a long time. What brings you here?"

Mike introduced Liam and said, "He is richer than me. So, you can realize how much money he has right?" They both laughed like they are going to steal Liam's wallet. Liam was confused. Then Mike said to that fat man, "Here is the thing. He is looking for something rough. Something hard-core. You know what I mean?"

The fat guy said, "Yeah, yeah. I know what you mean. I feel you dawg. So, you want some hard fuck, huh?"

Mike looked at Liam and Liam smiled a bit at Mike because that's exactly what Liam had in mind.

The fat man looked at Liam and said, "Shit negro, you look like that Zuckerberg dude. You his cousin?" Liam smiled and nodded no. He looked at Liam for a couple of seconds and said, "Holy shit man. You are that dude. That nigga that owns Hydro tech right?" Liam nodded, then the man said, "Damn man. I thought I recognized you. You are fully loaded. So, I will introduce the premium bitches to you, aight?" Liam smiled, and Mike laughed with the fat man.

Then the fat man said, "Follow me fellas. I will blow your mind."

They followed him. They went through two doors. After that, they entered a night club. It was an underground club. There were a lot of strippers in it. Most of them were fully naked. Most of the people inside that club were drunk or high on drugs. People were doing cocaine and heroin and it was not a big deal. Everyone was just minding their business. They didn't give a fuck about anyone else. Some were doing drugs, some were dancing, and some were just having sex around everyone. There was a DJ and he was playing loud techno music. But there was a lot of security around the club and they were always keeping track of what people were doing. If anyone tried to disturb anyone, the security would throw them out of the club and beat the shit out of them. It looked like it was an illegal club.

Then they went through another door. That hall was completely sound-proof so they could not hear one bit of that loud techno music from the other side. It was a bright room. Most people were wearing suits in it. There still were strippers that were half and full naked there, but it was obvious that it was a posh club. Liam thought that this was what that fat man was talking about, so he slowed down but Mike signaled him to follow him.

Then Liam came near Mike and asked him, "I thought this was it. This club looks fine to me." Then Mike said, "Just trust me. This is not it. There's something more. So, follow us and keep your voice down." They went through another door. In there, it was dark and there was a sofa in the middle of it. Then the fat man showed the sofa to Mike and Liam, indicating to them to take a seat on it.

The fat man said, "All right gentlemen, behind this curtain, there is a one-way mirror. You will see a couple of beautiful women. And they are willing to do anything for you. I mean ANYTHING. Hell, if you pay them well, they will even marry you without asking any questions. So, brace yourselves. Here they come."

He opened the curtain. There was a mirror and they could see the other side of it but the women wouldn't be able to see them. Then a door from the other side opened and a very beautiful woman walked through it. She was wearing a long red dress and had matching lipstick. Liam couldn't believe his eyes because she looked like a posh lady. Then the fat man started to introduce her to both Mike and Liam. He said everything about her: name, age, height, and weight. He even told them the age she lost her virginity, her bra size, how many plastic surgeries she had up to this point. He even said what she was not willing to do – which was nothing. He said that she was up to anything. Then he said the price for her, which was $50,000. If anyone pays that amount, they can take her home and do anything. It was like a slave auction. It took a couple of minutes for him to introduce her to both Mike and Liam. After he finished introducing her, he rang a bell. Then the second woman came in. She looked way too young to be a prostitute. The fat man said she turned 18 last week. Her prize was $70000.

Then like that, nine women came from that door. Liam's heart was pounding like a jet engine because he couldn't decide who to choose. Then in the middle of the introduction, Liam asked Mike, "How many women can I choose? I mean, I can't decide. I would like to take a couple because this kind of money is nothing to me."

Mike smiled at him and said, "Sorry bro. The rule is you can only choose one."

Liam started to think hard because he genuinely couldn't choose. He liked every woman behind that mirror. They were willing to do anything, and that just upped his excitement even more.

Then the fat man said, "This is your final contender. And she is a beauty." The final woman came through that door. Liam couldn't believe his eyes. She looked a lot like Ava. She had different hair and her face was a bit different than hers, but her body was exactly like Ava's. Even her face was more than 95% like Ava's. He couldn't believe his eyes. She was wearing a pearl white dress with no sleeves. It was a lot shorter and her panty was almost visible when she walked. Her cleavage was exactly like Ava's and her breasts were full of life and they jiggled when she walked. Liam slowly looked at Mike and even he noticed that. Liam could understand that by Mike's facial expression. Liam started to sweat like a pig. He couldn't understand why but it was because of his excitement.

The fat man said her age. She was a lot younger than Ava. Then he finally revealed her price. It was 1 million dollars. Liam was breathless because the rest of the women had so much lower prices than that. The maximum price was $150,000. It was like the whole thing was planned. Even Mike was surprised by that price. Then the fat man looked at Liam and asked, "Well, do you have a choice brother?"

"Why is the last woman expensive so much more than the rest?" Liam asked.

The fat man laughed and said, "Look around you brother. I own everything. I do a lot of business but in my years of experience. I learned that the most valuable business is information." Then he pointed his finger at his head indicating that he is smart. Liam couldn't understand what he meant by that. The fat man continued, "You see, Mr. Liam, your friend Mike is an old client of mine. I like him not because he is loyal to me but because he is rich, and he always introduces rich clients to me. When he said what you wanted last week, I did a little research and I found out that you are going to be my next client. So, I did a little digging about you. I found out about your ex-wife and what she did to you. I mean believe me, if some bitch did that to me, I would shoot that bitch in the head. After all, it was really easy to connect the dots. I found out what your ex-wife looked like and I found the perfect girl for you. So, this is Evangeline." Then the fat man said,, "Hell you could call her Eve or your wife's name, I don't give a fuck. But I know that you want her. Pay me upfront and you can have her and do anything with her."

Liam was speechless. He looked at Mike and he was speechless too. Then finally Mike said, "All I said was your name and what you want man." Liam could tell that Mike was telling the truth.

Liam replied, "That's what I want man. I mean I can spend 1 million for her. But I'm not sure what he promised in return."

The fat man heard that and said, "Well Mr. Liam, I can guarantee you that Eve will do anything for you. If you don't believe me, let me give you a little demonstration." Then he told his guard to bring Eve to the room. After she came into the room, Liam realized that she looked like Ava more than he thought. She had the same eyes as Ava. Then the fat man said, "Okay, Mr. Liam. What do you want her to do?"

Liam panicked. He never worked well under pressure and right now, everyone was looking at him including Eve. He couldn't figure out what to tell her. Then the fat man waited for a couple of seconds and said. "Well if you can't decide what to say, then I'll tell her." He went near Eve and whispered something to her. She smiled and opened her legs. Then she removed her panties without removing her dress. Then she squatted on the floor and defecated on it in front of everyone like it was not a big deal. There was no humiliation or confusion on her face at all. Liam was surprised by that. No one in the room made any noise when she did that. Then after she finished, she poked the shit with her finger. She put that finger in her mouth and started to lick all of the shit from her finger. Then she laid down and brought her face near the shit. She opened her mouth and put out her tongue. It was like she was about to eat the shit from the floor. There was no hesitation in her. But before she started to eat her own shit, Liam managed to speak up. He said, "That's enough. I mean she is a human being for Christ sake." Then she stopped and looked at Liam. Then she looked at the fat man and he signaled her to get out of there. She took her panty and went out of the room after winking at Liam. He was stunned by what happened.

The fat man came to him and said, "Well, what do you think mister? You saw that right. What she did was nothing to her. She enjoyed eating her own shit. Can you think of anything that she wouldn't do for you? She will do anything you command. She will be your personal slave. Kind of like a slave bitch without all the bullshit like crying and attention-seeking and shit."

Then Liam said, "So, you are telling me that I can do anything to her if I bought her from you?"

The fat man replied, "Anything brother. All your fantasies and desires will come to life. You might have to buy her expensive shit from time to time. But you won't have to pay her a cent. That's my guarantee. So, do we have a deal?"

Then Liam started to think. He really wanted her because she was exactly what he needed. So, he asked Mike about what he thought about the whole situation. Mike said, "It's your choice man. If you buy her, then she's yours."

So, Liam decided to buy her. When he told the fat man about his decision, he laughed with happiness and said, "Awesome. Then let's get down to business gentlemen."

They went to his office. After all of them sat down, Liam asked, "Oh shoot, I don't have that kind of money on me right now. What should I do now?"

The fat man laughed as usual and said, "Damn negro, this is the twenty-first century. You can pay me with your card," and he pulled out a payment machine. It was so damn convenient for Liam.

When he was about to pay the man, he remembered something. Then he said, "What about after?"

"After what?" the fat man asked.

Liam said, "After I'm done with her. I mean it's not like I'm going to marry her or anything. After I finally am satisfied, what should I do with her? Should I return her?"

The fat man laughed and said, "Hell nah brother. After you are done with her, you can do anything. You can kick her out or even give her a job at your company. I heard she is a good Java programmer."

"Are you kidding me? If she is good at programming, why the hell would she do something like this?"

The fat man said, "Well, the money is so good in this. And to be honest, she really does enjoy eating her own shit. So, don't feel bad about this okay. You can do whatever the fuck you want to her. The sky is the limit," and he winked at Liam.

Liam smiled and paid the man.

The fat man shouted, "Eve," and she came to the room wearing different clothing. She was wearing office attire. She was wearing a black coat and a short skirt and black heels. Then he said to Eve, "Ok baby. This is Mr. Liam. He is your new boss now. You will do anything and everything he tells okay."

She said "Oki dokz," and that was it. Liam now owned Eve.

Mike and Liam left with Eve. On the ride, Liam didn't say a word because he was freaking out. On the other hand, Mike managed to talk with Eve and get as much information out of her as possible. She said that she was born in China. It explained the Chinese look she had just like Ava. Also, she said that only her mother is Chinese. Her father was from Canada. She moved to Canada with her family when she was only three years old. Then she moved to the United States by herself when she was just 18 years old because she wanted to learn programming. After she graduated, she found Lucas. He is that black fat man. She then told them everything she knew about Lucas. He was not just a pimp; he had his hands on everything from drugs and guns to human trafficking. Most of the prostitutes he had are girls he got directly from China and India. Most of these girls didn't even know how to speak English, they just wanted asylum in America. They didn't know what was waiting for them on the other side. So, they had no choice but to work for Lucas when they arrived in America. Then Mike asked why Eve chose to work for Lucas if she had a degree in computer science and she never needed money that bad.

She responded, "Well, I was a nympho back then. Still is by the way." She winked at Liam. A nympho means she is a girl that has uncontrollable sexual desires. In other words, she is horny all the time, so this was the perfect job for her. Then she said, "So, this was the perfect job for me you know. I mean I always was into some freaky stuff. And Lucas provided me the platform for all of that. Plus, the money is always good you know. So, I had no reason to not do this. And for me, this was not like for other girls. I could always get out of this. But now, it looks like I'm stuck with you." She touched Liam's shoulder from the back seat.

Mike said, "Damn girl. That is quite a story. Looks like Liam is in for a treat, eh." Then he looked at Liam and smiled.

Liam returned the smile and turned to look at Eve. She winked at him while sucking her thumb like it was a penis. Liam's heart started to pound because he knew that he couldn't disappoint Eve. Maybe the reason Ava left him because girls usually like bad boys. So, he knew that he had to be rough with this woman in order to satisfy her needs. It looked like that she would not be impressed by money but only by sex, so he knew that he needed to up his sex game.

Mike dropped both of them at Liam's house and Liam took Eve inside. The house was full of his old photos. In most of them, he was with Ava. Eve took up one photo and looked at Ava for a couple of seconds and said, "Damn, Lucas told me about your ex-wife. But I had to see it with my own eyes. He was not wrong. She looks a lot like me." She started to think for a couple of seconds and said, "Well you know what, how about I look exactly like her." Liam raised his eyebrows in confusion, so Eve said, "I mean think about it. If I had a couple of minor plastic surgeries and get my hair straighten and blonde, I could look a lot more like her. So, what do you think?" It was too much for Liam. Before a couple of hours, he would never imagine anything like that. But now, he has a chance to have someone who looks exactly like the love of his life.

Then he said, "Why not."

Eve said, "Ok then. I have a couple of contacts. I'll look into them." Then after a few seconds, she said "Do you want to fuck me right now or do you want to wait till I change to your ex-wife?"

Liam replied, "I'll wait," because he didn't want to rush things. Then she said okay, and he showed her rooms she could have. He had lots of extra rooms in the house, so he said she could choose any room she liked.

She chose one room and she said, "Well, I didn't bring any luggage, so I don't have anything to wear. Can I have something to wear darling?" He said, "No problem. I have some of my wife's old clothes. I'll grab you one. Why don't you go and have a hot bath?"

He showed her the bathroom. Each bedroom had a bathroom adjacent to it. After she went inside the bathroom, Liam ran to the other room and tried to find suitable clothes for Eve. He found a t-shirt and shorts from his wife's old clothing collection. He put them on the bed inside Eve's room and he went to the living room and waited until she came outside. While he was waiting, Mike called him and asked, "So, did you fuck her yet?"

Liam said no to that and said he is taking his time because there is no rush and he wanted to take things slow.

Mike replied, "Screw that bro. This is not a relationship. Take dominance and fuck her brains out before it's too late."

Then Eve came out of the room wearing the clothes Liam had placed on her bed. She looked a lot like Ava and Liam had this tingling feeling when he saw Eve in the clothes. It was love. He knew right then and there that he is falling for her. He then realized that it would only end in pain because he could never be with a person like Eve. But it was too late to turn around. He said to himself that he would not get attached to Eve. He would just fuck her until he gets fed up with her and then just leave her like trash.

Eve went downstairs and had coffee by herself. She didn't say a word to Liam because she noticed how he was looking at her. She knew that she was special to Liam already. Then she said good night and went to her room.

Liam started to think. If this a good idea and what's going to happen to him if he starts to love her? What if she is not what was promised? Then he decided to take his time instead of being done with Eve as soon as possible. He went to sleep, hoping for a better tomorrow.

The next morning, Liam woke up around 7 o'clock. When he came to the living room, Eve had made coffee and breakfast for him. He was stunned. He never thought that she would do something like that for him. He had something completely different in mind when he bought her from Lucas. He was looking for a prostitute to have sex with. Instead, it looks like he got a brand-new wife. Then he said good morning to her and had the coffee. It was on point. For breakfast, she had made pancakes with syrup. He took a bite and he realized that it was the best pancake he has ever had. Because of his wealth, he has tried some of the world's best pancakes, but this was way better than any of them. Liam couldn't believe that Eve cooked them. Ava had never cooked food for him or even made coffee because she didn't know how to. She always used a servant to do that. One time, she tried to cook for Liam for his birthday and the food tasted like shit. With Eve, it's the complete opposite. He didn't ask for breakfast. She did that on her own and she did it marvelously. It was like he had stumbled upon an angel that had fallen from heaven.

Then he said, "Wow Eve, this is the best pancakes I have ever had. Where did you learn to cook like this?"

She smiled and said, "Well, I learned to cook from my mom. There are secret ingredients that we use in China. So, I added a little something and something and Voilà, this is what you get. Do you like it?"

"Like it? I love it. Damn I could eat this whole day."

"Ah, I have to tell you. I made an appointment for today with my plastic surgeon. I told him what I needed. I might need around $15,000 for the whole procedure. Are you fine with that?"

Liam said no problem because that was nothing to him. Later that day, she went to see the doctor by herself. Liam insisted that he would go with her, but Eve wanted the result to be a surprise. So, after she went for her appointment, she sent the account details to Liam so he could pay the doctor. She said to Liam to wait for a couple of days until the procedure was completed. Liam met Eve on Friday night and she went to see the surgeon on Saturday morning. On Sunday, Liam didn't get any messages or calls from Eve so he got worried. Then on Monday, when he went to the office, he gave a call to Eve, but she didn't pick up. Then that night, she sent a message to Liam saying, "The surgery was a success. But I will have to rest for a couple of days. And I can't talk because of the after-effects of the process. C u later, love Eve." He was relieved and got happy because she wrote "love."

Then he waited until Friday. She never called him, only texted him. She didn't even text him much. It's only one or two texts per day. So, he got worried and called Mike and told him what happened and Mike contacted Lucas for him. Lucas told Liam, "Don't worry brother. Bitch is just trying to impress you. If she leaves you, I'll bring that bitch to you in one piece. So, don't worry about it." Liam told Lucas not to hurt her. Then he laughed and said, "I don't have to hurt her because I trust her, so should you."

That made Liam a bit calm. Then he thought of waiting a bit longer. Then on Friday night, he had a party. When he was about to leave, someone knocked on the door. At that time, Liam was at his house alone by himself. At first, he thought it was his Uber driver, so he shouted, "Wait!" and got ready quickly and opened the door. It was Ava. She was just standing there and smiling. Liam hasn't seen her in months after their divorce because he refused to see her out of disgust and pure hate. He froze when he saw her.

Then she said, "Can I come in?" He tried to say something but no sound came out of his mouth. he said, "Thank you," and went inside.

He closed the door and took a deep breath and said, "What are you doing here, huh?"

She wore confusion on her face and started to think for a second to come up with a suitable answer for that. Then she asked, "What do you mean?"

Liam said, "How could you come here after everything you did to me? Do you know how humiliating that was, huh? You destroyed me. You fucked me to my core and left me to die." She looked at him for a couple of seconds and started to laugh like a crazy person. Liam got furious about that laugh because he thought that she was mocking him. Then she said, "Can't you recognize me?"

Liam was totally confused. He said, "What? Of course, I can recognize you, you cunt."

Then she said, "It's me, Eve. Not your ex-wife."

Liam was blown away by that. He could have sworn that it was Ava. He loved her since he was a kid. He fantasized about her until he got her. Even after that, she was all he could see when he closed his eyes. He could remember every physical detail about Ava. Her eyes, her face, even every little flaw of her was something that Liam was so familiar with. He could imagine her 100% accurate after closing his eyes. That's how much he remembered Ava. So, there is no way that he could mistake Eve for her. Before, Eve looked a lot like Ava, but the difference was so obvious, especially for Liam. But now, she looks exactly like Ava. Even Liam couldn't tell the difference.

It was amazing. This was a feeling that Liam hadn't felt in a long time.

Eve turned around a couple of times so Liam could see her at every angle. Then she asked, "What do you think?"

Liam said, "I can't believe it. I won't believe it. It's impossible. How could you be Eve when you look exactly like Ava?"

"Well, that's the beauty of plastic surgery sweety. So, why don't we take this for a spin? I want to go out with you today and see how many people recognize me as your ex." Then Liam agreed with her at once because for him, it felt like he got his old life back.

They went to a night club. Mike was waiting for them at the entrance. When he saw Liam with Eve, he said, "What the fuck man? Why did you get back again with this fucking whore?" Then Liam smiled and whispered to him the truth. He couldn't believe it at first. Then she had to tell him what she had to do to convince Liam a week ago, which was that eating her own shit scenario. Only then Mike was able to believe that it was really Eve. Then Liam said that they want to check how many would mistake Eve for Ava. Then he made a bet with Mike. He said that if anyone figured out that it's not Ava, he would give Mike 1,000 dollars. Mike agreed to it because he really hated Ava for what she did to Liam. Then they went to the club. It was not a usual club. It was a club for very rich people. So, they could do anything in it, and the crowd was familiar for both Liam and Mike because they are regulars for this club. Eve acted like Ava the whole time and no one realized that it was not Ava. She kissed Liam a lot and acted like they were in love the whole time. She was the wife Liam desired all his life that day and he felt like he was back with a better version of Ava. He was genuinely happy after a long time. Even when he was with Ava, he had this huge doubt that she was with him for his money. But he didn't have that doubt when he was with Eve. Maybe it's because he believed that he owned her. Maybe he believed that Eve truly wanted to make him happy. But in the end, he was truly happy, and he really enjoyed the time at the club and no one had the slightest doubt about Eve. So, Liam won the bet against Mike. Instead of paying Liam $1,000, Mike agreed to pay the whole bill for the club for all three. It was a hell of a lot more than $1,000 but he also really enjoyed that time with Eve because he knew that it became a reality because of him. After all, he was the one who introduced Liam to Lucas.

Liam and Eve went home around midnight. After they went inside his house, Eve said "Okay animal, what do you want to do to me?" He was horny and drunk at the time. At first, he wanted to have rough sex with her and torture her but now it was like he had feelings for her. Now, he didn't want to hurt Eve at least a bit. So, he told that to her. She was disappointed because she wanted to have hardcore sex with him. So, she said, "Are you kidding me, you fucking pussy? You know who I am right? I'm your ex-wife bitch. I cheated on you when you loved me from the bottom of your heart. I never loved you back. I just wanted your money. I mean, look at you. Did you ever think that a dumb-looking pussy like you could ever get a woman like me, huh? Everyone knew what I wanted from you. But no one bothered to tell you that because no one cared about you and everyone thought that you are nothing but a fucking pussy. That's the truth, the whole truth and nothing but the truth. So, what are you gonna do about it, huh, you pathetic little cunt?"

She said those things because she wanted to focus on the hatred Liam had towards Ava so he would get angry with Eve and try to rape her. Liam also realized that but what Eve said really got through to him because he knew deep down that everything Eve said was completely true. But he tried his best not to snap. Then Eve said, "What are you waiting for you bitch ass motherfucker. Hit me. Don't be a pussy like you have always been. Rip my clothes off and get your revenge you fucking nerd."

Liam snapped. The turning point was calling him a nerd. He really hated that word. Everyone used to call him that and that was the main reason he lost his confidence his whole childhood and it led him to be afraid to ask Ava out when he was in high school. So, he had a lifelong grudge with that word. He snapped and went towards Eve with anger and tears in his eyes. They were not because of sadness but because of anger. Then Eve had a little smile on her face because that's exactly what she needed. So, she didn't try to calm Liam down or stop him. She just let it flow.

Liam grabbed her by her neck and started to strangle her. When she was about to faint, Liam quickly stopped and apologized. Eve said, "Did I tell you to stop?" Then Liam knew what he had to do. So, he slapped her in the face as hard as he could. It left his whole hand-print on her face. Then she said "again" so he slapped the other cheek the same way. Now, her whole face looked like an apple and tears fell from her eyes. But her lips were smiling because she was enjoying it deep down. Then she grabbed Liam by his collar and whispered, "My safe word is sea cucumber. If I say it, you stop. Otherwise, don't you dare stop, okay?" Liam nodded yes and picked her up and took her to his bedroom and threw her on the bed. Then he jumped on her and ripped her clothes off. He ripped her bra. He didn't bother to remove it properly, he just ripped it off of Eve's chest.

Eve's boobs were staring right at him. It was exactly like Ava's boobs. So, he started to remember the good times he had with her. Eve figured out in seconds that Liam was going down memory lane. So, she quickly responded, "These are the tits that cheated on you. So, punish them you fucking pussy." Liam came back on track. He remembered what Ava did to him. So, he grabbed her tits and started to squeeze them as hard as he could. Eve started to scream when he did that. But that scream was a combination of pain and pleasure. Liam realized that she was enjoying the pain. So, he squeezed them until her nipples started to drain a little bit of liquid and blood. Then he sucked her nipples as hard as he could. Eve slapped him on his head and said, "What are you waiting for? Bite them." Then he started to bite her nipples until he tasted blood. He leaned back and turned Eve downward. He ripped her panties off. Then he squeezed her ass cheeks and slapped them as hard as he could till they became so damn red. He removed his belt and started to whip her ass with it. After every whip, Eve screamed. But she didn't scream for help. She screamed, "Harder." So, Liam tried harder and harder to whip her ass as hard as he could but every time, she just said harder instead of the safe word. He realized that he couldn't whip her as hard as she wanted so he started to whip her back instead. She still didn't say the safe word. So, he turned the belt around and started to whip her back with the belt buckle instead. Then her screaming increased, but she didn't say harder. Instead, she started to moan. Liam realized that this was the amount of pain she wanted to endure. But because of the belt buckle, her back started to scratch and bleed. But he didn't want to stop because this is what Eve wanted and he didn't want to disappoint her.

After about 15 whips, she said sea cucumber. So, Liam stopped, and he was glad because he knew that he couldn't hurt her more. He turned her around and started to kiss her on the lips. Then suddenly, she bit his lips until they bleed. Liam backed off and touched his lips and saw the blood on his finger. Then Eve said, "Bite me, bitch." So, he kissed her again and bit her lips until they bled. He moved to her neck and started to lick and suck her neck. All the time she moaned and said, "Harder." Then he sucked her neck as hard until she got multiple hickeys. He slapped her on her hickeys to torture her more. Trailing his lips down her body, he started to lick her belly button. She had a piercing in her belly button. So, Liam bit it with his teeth and started to pull it out until it almost ripped her belly. She screamed, "Yes," when he did that. Then he went down on her and started to lick her pussy. He bit her clit while sucking it as hard as he could. Eve was screaming with pleasure the whole time. Then he inserted his middle finger inside her pussy and started to move it in and out. She said, "More fingers." Liam put another finger, but she screamed that she needed more. Then he put another, but she was not satisfied. He spat on her pussy and put four fingers inside her pussy and started to fuck her with them. Then Eve moaned, "Put your thumb also baby. I want all of it." Liam was not sure that her pussy could take it. But he had no choice because she wanted that. So, he inserted his thumb. At first, it was really hard because her pussy was super tight. But right after he managed to insert his thumb, Eve started to moan with satisfaction. He slowly inserted his hand inside her pussy up to his wrist. Then she said, "More baby more." Liam inserted more until he couldn't anymore.

Then Eve said, "Do the same to my asshole." Liam was stunned when she said that because he never thought that it would be possible. But he had to do it because Eve insisted. So, he slowly took his hand out. His hand was dripping in saliva and pre-cum from her pussy. So, he quickly put one finger inside her asshole. Then Eve said, "Put all of them at once." He tried to put all of the rest at once, but her asshole was super tight. But because his whole hand was so damn wet, he managed to put his whole hand inside Eve's asshole after she opened her ass cheeks. Liam got curious because he has never seen anything like this before. So, he started to penetrate her asshole with his fist superfast. Then Eve said, "Put your left fist inside my pussy at the same time." Liam spat on his left fist and put it at once inside her pussy while his right fist was already inside her asshole. The left fist went inside with ease because her pussy was already stretched and was super wet. Then he started to move his hand in both her asshole and pussy with both his fists. It was a whole new experience for him. Then Eve screamed, "Harder baby, I'm gonna cum." He increased his speed and suddenly, Eve's whole body started to shake like she was having a seizure. He looked at her face and saw that her eyes became white. She was climaxing. Liam didn't stop until she finished her climax. He saw that squirt was dripping from his right hand like a tap. He realized that she is a squirter and his fist was blocking the entire squirt. Otherwise, he would have been drowned in her squirt. Then he slowly took both his hands out. Both were completely wet and his righthand had some poop on them. He licked them a bit. It was better than he imagined. Then he put those fingers inside Eve's mouth as deep as he could and command her to suck them. He slaps her on the cheeks and ass cheeks while he was doing it. He did that because he knew that Eve was enjoying it.

He removed the rest of his clothes. Then he got on top of her and whispered, "I'm going to fuck your brains out." He put his dick inside her pussy. It went with ease because her pussy was completely wet, and it was expanded due to all the fisting. But it was tight enough for him, but it looked like Eve was not enjoying the fucking. It made Liam so mad. So, he slapped her tits and squeezed her nipples until they bleed. He was so horny at that time, so he really wanted Eve to enjoy him fucking her.

Then he leaned in and sucked her tits. Then Eve said, "Choke me, Daddy." So, he leaned back and put his right hand on her neck and started to choke her. He saw that she was enjoying it. It gave him the boost he needed. He put his other hand on top of her neck and started to strangle her with both his hands. He increased the speed of his fucking while he was strangling her. Then he strangled her as hard as he could. He saw her face was becoming bluish. She was saying something. He leaned to her and heard the words, "Sea cucumber." He knew that she couldn't breathe but he couldn't stop. He was so horny and was about to cum. So, he said, "Just a little baby. Hold still." Then he strangled her as hard as he could and increased his speed to the fullest. Then after about 20 seconds, he came inside her pussy and it was the best orgasm he has ever had. He moaned a lot when he was climaxing. After that, he removed his hands from her neck and laid down on her. Then he waited for a couple of minutes to catch his breath.

He said, "What do you think babe?" but Eve didn't respond. So, he got up and looked at her. Her eyes were opened but she wasn't breathing. He knew right then and there that he went too far with her. So, he tried to give her CPR, but she didn't start to breathe. Then he panicked and dialed 911. But before sending the call, he figured that he would go to jail since this looked like a rape scene. So, he quickly called Mike instead and told him what happened. He told Liam to calm down and he would take care of it. He told him to stay put and don't talk to anyone. Then Mike came to Liam's house after a couple of minutes. He saw the room. Then he said, "Fuck me man. What did you do to her?" Eve's back was full of blood from all the whipping he did and her nipples were also bleeding. Both her asshole and pussy were stretched so anyone could tell that someone had inserted something large inside them.

Then after a couple of minutes, Lucas came with a couple of guys. When he saw the room, he said, "Damn man, you are some nasty ass motherfucker. To be honest, I thought she would survive longer than that." Liam got confused because it felt like Lucas knew that this was going to happen. Then Lucas said, "Don't worry bro. I'll take care of this. Usually, this happens most of the time. I'm sure you didn't mean that but because of you, this girl is dead. So, that's on you. Don't tell the cops anything. If you do that, I will personally put a bullet in your head, aight?" Then Liam nodded yes but he knew that he couldn't live with it. Tears were dripping from his eyes but there was nothing he could do. Then Lucas's goons sealed Eve's body and took it away. Lucas said, "Pleasure doing business with you," and left. Then Mike said that he has to go with him to make sure that the body is disposed of properly. After he left, Liam was at his house all alone. His arms were sweaty, and he couldn't breathe properly. He sat down on his bed and started to cry because he lost the only chance where he could feel happy again before even trying it.

Mike followed them in his car and then Lucas called him and told him not to follow them, so he had to stay behind. One of Lucas's goons removed the seal and Eve woke up and said, "Wow, that was fast." Lucas laughed and said, "One million dollars for a week of work, huh? Not bad." It was a total con to get money from Liam. She was just acting dead and since Liam was panicked at the time, he didn't realize that she was faking her death.

THE END

02

The Girl With An Addiction

Jacob was a low-level drug dealer. He always had his specific corner and all he had to do was sell drugs to those who come to him. Then he gives all the money to his boss every night and in return, he gets a 20% cut from the money. It's for his service and risk he takes to sell the drugs. He knew that what his boss was earning in a day was more than what he could earn in a year. But there was nothing he could do because it's all about who's the boss and who owns the most territory in the city. His boss was the biggest gangster in the city, and everyone was afraid of him. His name was Whack Jack. He got his name because he always whacks everyone who gets in his way. Whack means killing or stabbing, so everyone knew that they should not cross Whack Jack ever. Even Jacob was so afraid of him. Still, he worked for him on his corner for almost a year, so he was able to gain Whack Jack's trust at this level.

Jacob had everything on him. He had heroin, crystal meth, molly and weed. He even had prescribed drugs such as Amphetamines, Adderall, and Valium. So, everyone around him knew that Jacob was the man they needed when they wanted to get high. Also, his prices were always fair. He didn't increase his price when the demand increased. Instead, he got more supplies. So, all his customers trusted him.

Jacob's street name was Hunk. It's because he had a foot-long dick and his ex-girlfriend bragged to all her friends about how huge his dick was and how he managed to fuck her until she squirts and how awesome his dick was. That's how he got that street name. Even though no one else has seen his dick, people assumed that it was really big. It was like a legend or a myth among the streets. All his customers joked or genuinely asked to see his dick. Most times, Jacob would laugh but sometimes he gets angry because everyone asked about his dick all the time. It's like everyone is obsessed with his dick and only with his dick. But because of his nickname, he got girls with ease. He didn't even have to try. Girls came to him and tried to seduce him because no woman could resist a big black cock. He liked that a lot but the downside of it was that when he had sex with girls like that, he had to pleasure them because he thought that they deserved that pleasure since they approached him. So, most of the time he didn't enjoy it much. Almost all women couldn't have his whole dick inside their pussy. Most of the time, he could only put less than half of his dick inside. So, it was hard for him to fully enjoy the sex with these women. But women always enjoyed it to the fullest, so they always wanted more but Jacob tried to avoid them since it was not much enjoyable for him. So mostly, he had one-night stands.

When it came to business, he always wanted cash upfront from his customers. He would never loan drugs to others. He would never get anything other than money in return. Some tried to give him sporting event tickets or gold watches or old shits instead of money, but he would never accept them. He also had a pistol with him at all times for protection, but he never had to fire it at all. Jacob was a smart man, not just street smart. He was genuinely smart, and Whack Jack knew that. Jacob even went to college, but he didn't graduate since he couldn't pay tuition because he was an orphan and couldn't find a proper part-time job. That's when he met his former boss Al Diddy. He was a low-level thug, but he was the one who got Jacob to the drug business. Al Diddy got his name because he loved former world-class gangsters and rappers. So, it's a combination of Al Capone and P. Diddy. Al Diddy gave Jacob the opportunity when he needed money the most. Then he realized that he could go nowhere with college, so he decided to drop out of college and join Al Diddy's gang. It was the biggest decision he had to make in his life. He knew it was the wrong decision, but he had no choice but to make it. It was a practical solution for him. At first, he did deliveries for Al Diddy. Then Al Diddy realized that Jacob was a smart guy, so he moved Jacob up the ladder. He became the right-hand man for Al Diddy. He knew everything about the drug business but then Al Diddy died from a car accident, so Jacob had no choice but to join another gang. That's when he met Whack Jack. His gang was far more big and violent than Al Diddy's gang. At first, he was uncomfortable, but Whack Jack knew Jacob's potential. He knew that Jacob was smart and loyal to his former boss, so he made sure that Jacob always had a place in his gang. He managed to climb up the ladder within Whack Jacks gang also. But then he had to kill a man to prove his loyalty to Whack Jack. Even though Jacob had done a lot of bad things, he had never killed a man before. So, he was not able to prove his loyalty to Whack Jack. Then he got demoted to a street-level dealer. That's how he ended up in that street corner. But he was fine with it. The money was good for him and the risk was minimal. He knew all the cops that were on his street and he managed to give them a fair cut so they would look the other way. Since he worked for Whack Jack, no one would dare to cross him, so he had no problem with other thugs as well.

But one time, he had a serious incident with a rivalry gang. Jacob was minding his business on his corner and a group of thugs came in a white van and suddenly kidnapped him. Then they put him in a dark room for a couple of days and tortured him. They wanted to know details about Whack Jack's drug operation, but Jacob didn't tell them anything. He did it not because he was loyal to Jack but because he knew what Jack would do to him if he gave that information up. Their leader was a cousin of Al Diddy called Narkos. He knew Jacob back in the day. So, at first, he gave a chance to Jacob to give up the information. But when he refused, Narkos decided to torture him, despite the relationship they had back in the day. That's when Jacob realized that he could never trust anyone in the drug business.

He said, "I won't give you any information because I know if I give you what you want, I'm a dead man. So, torture me all you want. But I won't give you what you want."

Narkos said, "I admired you Jacob. But the thing is, everyone has a limit. It's just a matter of time till I find yours. After that, you would beg me to kill you. So, just wait."

Then Narkos let his goons torture him. At first, they just punched him. But then, they started to break his fingers one by one. The main man who tortured him was Smiley. He had this nickname because he always smiled. He was a huge muscular man, so Jacob had no chance of fighting him even if he was not tied up to a chair. Smiley laughed all the time when he tortured Jacob. When Jacob was screaming, he laughed like it was a turn on for him. It was a turn-on for him because Jacob noticed Smiley always had a boner when he was torturing him.

Smiley said, "I was in the army and I had two tours to Afghanistan. My specialty was torturing. I managed to get everything out of any terrorist we captured. They called me the master of torture because I never failed. So, believe me when I tell you this Jacob, I will break you. But I will take my time. So, I encourage you to not give up because I want you to fight. Fight through the pain as much as you can so I can use every technique I know to hurt you."

He broke his fingers one by one using a hammer. Jacob realized that they were holding him under a meat farm because of the smell. Therefore, they had all the equipment they needed to torture him. But still, Jacob didn't give anything up. The truth was he knew nothing. But he knew that if they knew that he knew nothing, they would simply kill him. So, it was the only leverage he had to stay alive.

Then Smiley put sticks in his nails. He did it very slowly so Jacob would feel the pain to the fullest. He always made sure that Jacob was fully hydrated and had a full stomach. He said, "You won't pass out if you eat well. So, if you don't pass out, you will feel all the pain." He also gave him an injection so he would not pass out. Then Smiley removed his nails one by one. He used the same metal sticks he put inside his nails to remove the nails. Then he removed a couple of his front teeth and put salt on them. Then he electrocuted Jacob's balls. Still he didn't tell them that he didn't know anything. Then Smiley put gun powder in Jacob's anus and lit. It was the most painful moment in Jacob's life. He passed out the moment Smiley literally light his asshole on fire. Then when he woke up, he was not tied up and he was alone in the room. He couldn't think straight for a moment because of the pain. But then he managed to get out of the room. Smiley had left without tying him up. He didn't even close the door because he didn't think that Jacob would wake up that quickly and he had gone out to smoke some crack. Then Jacob saw a small door that had an exit sign above it. When he exited the building, he knew where he was. It was just a couple of blocks away from his corner. He quickly called Whack Jack from a nearby payphone and told him what happened. Luckily, he had some coins left in his pockets. But before he finished, Smiley found him and threw him out of the phone booth. He started to beat him up so bad, Jacob vomited blood. Smiley broke his ribs and his left leg so Jacob couldn't fight back. Even if he could, there was no chance that he could ever defeat a big ass muscular, hyper tense man like Smiley. After he finished beating Jacob up, he said, "You won't walk again. I will make sure of that later. I'll cut off your feet so slowly, you will feel every inch of your legs being detached from your body." Then he picked up Jacob like it was nothing even though he was 6 feet tall and weight almost 200 pounds. Before he could walk 10 steps, he fell. Jacob barely had it together at that moment. He was trying his best not to faint. So, his hearing was not good at the time. That's why he couldn't figure out why Smiley fell. Then he saw that blood was coming from Smiley's head. Whack Jack came to him and said, "Don't worry bro. I got you." Jacob saw that he came with an army and they raided that building. He heard gunshots and screams at first, then he passed out.

After a while, he woke up and a sexy nurse was attending to him. She was giving him a sponge bath. Then he asked, "What happened?"

The nurse said, "Well, Mr. Whack found you when you were almost beaten to death. They couldn't have taken you to a hospital since you are a gangster and you had so much shit happened to you, so he brought you here to get better." He asked where he is. She responded, "Well, you are at Mr. Whack's house. Don't worry. Everything will be fine. I promise."

When he looked at his body. Most of it was bandaged completely. He felt a little dizziness but no pain at all. Then Whack Jack came to the room and said, "Heyyy. This is the man of the day. How are you hunk Jacob?" Jacob nodded. Then Whack Jack said, "Well, the doctor told me what they did to you. It's pretty fucked up man. I mean they literally lit your ass on fire and that was fucking biblical negro." Then he laughed. Jacob tried to laugh with him, but he couldn't because when Whack Jack talked about it, he remembered how it felt and it was so damn painful for him. Whack Jack said, "Don't worry bro. We killed everyone and saved the boss for you. He is being tortured at the moment. When you get better, you will get the chance to put a bullet in his head. So, get better fast. You are the most loyal guy I have. I mean no one would have had your limits. Even I would have given up before getting my ass on fire. But you....you didn't give anything up. I underestimated you, brother. But not anymore. After you get back on your feet, I want you to be my right-hand man."

After a couple of days, Jacob managed to get back on his feet. Whack Jack gave him a couple of pure gold teeth to replace the teeth that Smiley removed when he was being tortured. His nails were beginning to heal and his asshole burn was healed almost completely. He managed to stop taking his pain killers. So, his dizziness and side effects were gone at the moment. Then Whack Jack took him to the basement. Since they managed to take Narkos alive, they have been torturing him the whole time Jacob was recovering. They did exactly everything that they did to Jacob to Narkos in that same order. They have removed his nails and broke his fingers. They have even pulled Narkos' teeth exactly like how they have pulled

Jacob's teeth. They also burned his asshole using the same method. By that time, Narkos was half dead.

Whack Jack said, "This is all about sending a message. If someone tries to fuck with me, I fuck back with balls." Then he took a huge knife and cut Narkos' balls off. Narkos started to scream in agony while Whack Jack and his goons laughed hard. Jacob was stunned at that moment. He was afraid but at the same time he wanted Narkos to suffer for what he did to him. The only reason he was not satisfied with this scenario was because Whack Jack couldn't capture Smiley alive. Jacob wanted him to suffer more since he was the one who personally tortured him the whole time even though Narkos just gave the order. Then after a minute, Narkos started to faint. Whack Jack slapped him and told one of his goons to drop a bucket of water on his head so he wouldn't pass out. But it was clear for Jacob that he was going to bleed to death because blood was dripping from where his balls used to be like a freaking hose. After they dropped a bucket of water on him, he woke up again, but he didn't even have the energy to scream. Then Whack Jack said, "That's good. I think it's time for you to meet your maker." He gave a pistol to Jacob and said, "Shoot him in the head."

Jacob was frozen at that moment. He had so much anger toward Narkos. He wanted to kill him, but he had never killed anyone before, so it made him freeze.

Whack Jack gave Jacob the gun by force. He couldn't even hold it straight because most of his fingers were still broken. His hands were shaking a lot because of that and also because he was afraid. But after a few seconds, he managed to point the gun at Narkos' head. Then Whack Jack said, "Pull the trigger," but Jacob hesitated. Whack Jack realized that, but he wanted Jacob to pull the trigger. So, he said, "Pull the fucking trigger, you pussy. He destroyed you. He deserves it. So, pull the god damn trigger motherfucker. Just pull it right now."

Jacob closed his eyes tightly and pulled the trigger. Then everyone went quiet. Jacob slowly opened his eyes. He shot Narkos in his left eye. He was dead on that chair. Then everyone cheered.

Whack Jack said, "Welcome back my right-hand man," then he hugged Jacob.

This is how he managed to become the second most powerful man in Whack Jack's gang. With that post, he gains the utmost respect among his gang. Also, he got famous among other gangs because he was someone who managed to suffer pain from Smiley at its most but still didn't gave up. So, he didn't have to work on his corner anymore. Jacob bought a new bigger and better apartment. Also, he had two gang members as his personal security at all times. They stayed with him 24/7. He never killed anyone else after the incident with Narkos. He always tried to avoid violence at all costs. But sometimes, he had to be violent in order to maintain his reputation. But even when he did that, he managed to do that without killing anyone.

He stayed at his new apartment for more than a year. During that time, he managed to get lots of girls. He knew that he could not have sex when his bodyguards were around. So, he bought the apartment next to his so his bodyguards would stay there during the night, especially when he brought girls to his apartment. He liked everything about his apartment except for one thing. He had new neighbors next door. They were a young couple. They were so loud and always fighting with each other. It was disturbing for him because they fought until midnight most nights. It was a huge turn off for him when he brought girls to his apartment. Sometimes, he even used his bodyguard's apartment when he brought girls over.

His bodyguards were so loyal to him. Their names were David and James. Both of them were African Americans. Most of Whack Jack's gang had black guys. His bodyguards insisted that they would do something about that couple, but Jacob said to leave them be because he didn't want to bring unwanted heat upon himself. Then one day, they didn't fight. They didn't fight for a week. So, Jacob got curious. He said to David and James to check what's up with that couple. Then after they checked, they came and said, "The man had died. Now, it's just the girl. I gotta tell you, man, she is one hell of a pretty junky. I mean you gotta see that man." Then Jacob got curious, so he went there the next morning. He wanted to introduce himself as her neighbor.

He went and knocked on the door, but no one came. Then he knocked again, and he heard a scream saying, "Wait just a god damn second." She came and opened the door. She had a really angry face but the second she saw Jacob, her anger vanished in thin air and she smiled. Jacob froze also when he saw her because she was really beautiful and that was not what he was expecting. She was super thin, but she had large boobs. Her boobs were so big for her body but in a really good way. She was wearing a gray color sports bra and pink shorts. It was so short, it looked like a panty, so her entire legs were showing. Her entire body was completely shaved and was completely flawless except she had injection marks on her left elbow. It was so obvious because the rest of her body was perfect in every way. Jacob never found white women attractive but there was something different about this girl. Even though she was an obvious junky, she looked so damn innocent. Her lips were like an angel's. She had no makeup on whatsoever but still, she looked stunning like a model. She had long black hair. It was wavy and was up to her waist. She had light blue eyes that looked like a pair of diamonds.

It took Jacob a couple of seconds to admire her beauty and get back to the real world. Meanwhile, she was looking at him while rolling her hair and biting her lips. It was so damn obvious that she was attracted to Jacob because of the way she was looking at him. Then finally, he managed to build up the courage to talk to her.

"Hi, my name is Jacob and I live next door."

"Hi Jacob. I'm Olivia," then she shook his hand.

Jacob noticed that her hands were smooth like flowers. He had never touched any girl that had hands that smooth. She was rolling her hair with the other hand when she shook his hand and she was shaking her legs like a child because she was shy.

Then Jacob said, "I heard your husband died recently. My sympathy."

She said "Oh hell no. He was just a friend of mine. But thanks anyway."

Jacob didn't know what to say because it was not the answer he was hoping for. He knew that he was afraid to talk to her. He felt like he was back in college. He was shy to talk to girls back then. But now he is a well-reputed gangster who had a lot of sex with a lot of girls, so he had no shyness toward women. But with Olivia, it was different. It was then he realized that he was attracted to her so much.

She said, "Oh, how rude of me. Please come in." She moved away from the door so Jacob could go inside. Then she showed him a chair. After he sat down, she said, "Forgive me for what I'm wearing. I didn't expect any guests today." She tried to cover her cleavage with her hands out of pure shyness.

"Oh no. what's wrong with your clothes? They look so sexy to me," he smiled like an idiot. Then he saw Olivia's face turn red.

Then she asked, "Would you like a beer?"

"Sure. Why not."

She went inside and brought two beers and offered him one. She forgot to pull it. So, she said, "Oh sorry. Let me pull that for you."

Jacob responded, "No problem. I can do it." He pulled it open with his mouth. Since his front teeth were gold, it was nothing for him.

Olivia was so damn impressed by it. She said, "Wowee, can you do mine also," and started to cheer him on like a teenage girl. He was embarrassed but also felt special, so he did the same to her beer while looking at her. He wanted to impress her. He winked at her after he pulled the container. Then he offered her the beer and both of them sat down.

She asked, "So Jacob, what do you do for a living?"

It was obvious that he was a gangster because of his looks. He always wore clothing typical gangsters wore and had long dreads. Also, because of his gold teeth, no one could think otherwise. But she asked that any way to start a conversation.

He answered with his usual bullshit answer. He said, "Well, I'm an entrepreneur. I have a couple of businesses going on at the moment."

"Wow. I like that. I like it when a man doesn't depend on any big corporates and the government."

"So, what do you do Olivia?"

"Well, I'm an artist. But it won't pay as much. But that's my passion."

Jacob got curious. He always liked artists because he wanted to be an artist when he was a kid, but he had no artistic skills whatsoever. So, it was a dead dream for him but still, he had a lot of respect for other artists. He said, "Wow seriously. That's awesome. I always wanted to be an artist when I was a kid but I suck at it." He wanted to see her art so he said, "I know this is a bit forward but I'd really like to see some art you did." She smiled and said, "Well, of course. How thoughtful of you. But I have to warn you. My art is somewhat mmm unusual or some would say maybe weird."

Jacob said, "Well if you think about it, all art is weird at some point. That's what makes it unique, you know." That comment brought a smile to her face. Her face got red again because she was so happy because of that comment.

So, she said, "Well, wait here. I'll be back in a second." She ran inside a room and came back with a big board. She asked, "Are you ready Jacob?" He nodded yes. Then she showed him the painting.

It was a painting of a fruit basket, but the color scheme was highly unusual. Most of the fruits were brown. Some were a bit yellow and there was an apple in it. It was red but it was really dark red. But it was beautiful.

"Wow, it's so pretty. Did you draw it?" She nodded yes. Then he said, "To be honest, the color scheme is a bit unusual. But I think that's what makes it special, right?" She smiled and looked down. She was shy but Jacob couldn't understand why she would be shy by that comment. Then he asked, "Why would anyone think that your art is weird. It looks normal to me."

Then she looked down and said, "Well how can I put this... I'm someone who is considered a scat artist." She then looked at Jacob, but he had no idea what the fuck that meant. So, he looked at her strangely and it was obvious for Olivia that he did not understand. So, she said, "Well, what can you tell me about these colors? Are there any similarities in the color scheme?" Then he looked at it again and studied it. Then he came closer to the painting. While he was coming closer to it, he said, "Well, most colors are brownish. And the whole painting has very dark and dry colors. Even the red color looks so dry." Then he came near the painting and noticed the smell. He was able to connect the dots in seconds. The painting smelled like shit, literally. Then he understood what she meant by scat artist. She had done this painting using shit. Then he moved back a bit because he was genuinely disgusted by it. But he made sure that Olivia would not notice the fact that he was disgusted by her painting.

She noticed that after he smelled the painting, he knew what it was made of. Then she said "I used my own poop to make this painting. Everything in this painting came from me and only me. So, in a way, this painting is a part of me." Then she smiled like she was so proud of that fact.

He looked at the painting again and asked, "So, where did this red color come from? Did you use your own blood? That's some hardcore stuff, you know."

She smiled and said, "Well, the meaning of a scat artist is that you can't force things out of your body in order to make a painting so I didn't cut myself to get blood. This is just period blood. So, don't worry about it." She smiled and winked. It was more disgusting for him. Then she said, "I used my own urine to combine the colors instead of water. So, everything in this painting came out from one of my holes." Then she laughed. Jacob couldn't control his laughter because he knew that she was so damn right about that so he laughed too. Then she said, "That's the definition of a scat artist. You have to use your own poop to draw the painting. Most men don't go in this direction because they only have poop. But with us girls, we have period blood also. So, with two primary colors, we can make a lot of colors. If we had a proper diet, we can get yellow poop also. So, that means I can make any color I want out of things that come out of my body. How beautiful is that right?" It was kind of impressive even for Jacob. Even though he wanted to be an artist, he didn't know much about the subject. This was something he had never heard of or ever thought of. So, he finally understood why she did that. She wanted to make a painting out of her so that she could be art.

"Wow. I gotta say girl, I'm really impressed. You should keep doing this. I mean this is some serious art and shit."

She smiled and said, "Why do you speak like a gangster?" He had no answer for that because she asked that out of nowhere.

"Whaaat. That's racist. This is how all black people talk girl."

She smiled and said, "Oh, no, no, no. Don't pull that racist card on me okay. I know a lot of black guys and I know how they talk. There's a big difference between black talk and black gangster talk. You have black gangster talk." Then she smiled.

He knew that he couldn't hide the fact that he was a gangster. Even if he tried to speak like a normal person from that moment, it was obvious for anyone by Jacob's appearance because he had a typical gangster look.

"Well, it's that obvious, huh."

She said, "Yes. And you should not hide who you are. You should embrace that stuff because that's what defines you, you know. If you lie about that, then what is the truth about you? Everything becomes a lie at the end."

Jacob agreed with her not because he wanted to impress her but because he knew that she was 100% right. It was like she was a genius in a sexy disguise. Then she asked, "So what do you do, gangstah?"

"What do you mean what do I do?"

"Come, on man. You know what I'm asking. What do you do? Like what gangster stuff do you do? Do you do drug business or gun business or killing and stuff?"

Then he laughed and said, "Damn girl. This ain't a movie, aight. We don't just do killings and shit. And it is hard as shit to do gun business in this town. I just do little thug shit you know what I'm saying."

Then she touched him on his arm and said, "Come ooooon. Tell me. Don't be shy. I told you what I do. And I didn't hide a thing. Now it's your turn."

Jacob realized that when she touched his arm, she was impressed by his muscles. He knew that he had to give her something. So, he said, "Okay. I do a little bit of drug stuff. Not a lot. I just mostly deal with weed."

Then she said, "Good for you. So, the next time when I need weed, I'll call you." She winked at Jacob who smiled with embarrassment. He knew that he shouldn't tell someone he just met what he is doing for a living, but she caught him in a vulnerable moment.

"I should go now. I have to be somewhere." He said that not because he had to be anywhere but because he knew that if he stayed any longer, he will tell more about what he does to Olivia.

"Okay, gangster, be safe and drop by anytime you like." Before he went outside, she asked for his number. He gave it and went away.

That night while lying in bed, he started to think about her. He had never had feelings for a girl like that before. He knew he only preferred black girls but with Olivia, it was something different. He wasn't just attracted to her. He was falling for her and he knew that. She was pretty but he knew that she was a junky because the needle marks on her elbow were so fresh and obvious. He knew that if he started an affair with a junky, it would look bad and be bad for his business and for him. Since he had access to any drugs, it would not help Olivia. Then suddenly, he got a call from an unknown number. He always answered the phone from unknown numbers because lots of members in his gang use burner phones in case they get caught.

So, he answered the phone and from the other side he heard, "Are you Jacob the thug," with a weird rough but funny voice. He tried to recognize the voice, but he couldn't. Then he said, "Who the fuck is this bitch?"

The person laughed and then said, "I's me Olivia."

He quickly apologized for calling her a bitch even though he usually calls women bitches a lot. That was the moment he realized that he respected her.

Then she said, "I was thinking about you."

So, he knew that he had made a good first impression on her that morning. He smiled and said, "What were you thinking?"

"Why did you have gold teeth. I mean you must have had pretty teeth right. So, why did you replace them with something artificial?"

"To be honest, it's not by choice. I had an accident and all my front teeth got damaged because of it. So, that's why I replaced them with gold teeth. And hey, it's not all bad. Remember, I pulled the lid out of your beer bottle." Then they both laughed.

They spoke for about an hour. She said things about her past and the art she did. She spoke about her former boyfriend who fought with her a lot in that apartment. She said that even though she didn't consider him her boyfriend, they had sex because he was the one who gave her drugs. He also was the one who made her addicted to drugs. So, she had no choice but to endure the abuse because she was so addicted to heroin at that point. Then after he finally died, she was sober for a week. Jacob then congratulated her and wished her a speedy rehabilitation. Around midnight, they finished their first call.

After that, most nights Olivia would call him. If she didn't call, then Jacob always called her to check up on her. He started to go to her apartment to check up on her in the morning and he started to bring her coffee while doing that. She liked it and Jacob also enjoyed spending time with her. Olivia always stayed at her house because she was doing her paintings all day. After a while, Jacob got used to her scat paintings. One time he suggested that she should go out more. They started to go out for lunch on most days. They did it as friends because Jacob was afraid to ask her out. The reason for that was he never had to ask a girl out. All he wanted from girls was sex and they came to him to have sex. He never had to try even a bit. He also never had a proper affair with a girl before, so this was something completely new to him.

Olivia was attracted to Jacob also but she was waiting until Jacob made his first move. But he couldn't do it because he didn't know how to. They spend a lot of time with each other like this for about three weeks and they became so close. Jacob had become her new drug. When she was with him, she didn't need heroin or anything. Things were turning around for Olivia. When her ex died, she was broke but now because she stopped using drugs, she managed to save more money. Also, Jacob bought her lunch most days and it was also beneficial for her. He even told her what happened to him with Smiley and how he got gold teeth. It was painful for him to relive that moment, but it was worth it because after saying that, he even became closer to Olivia.

Then suddenly, she went missing. Jacob couldn't contact her. She left her phone in her apartment. He tried everything. First, he told his gang members to go look for her in every drug house because he thought she might relapse. He became afraid because he really cared about her and he wanted to find her so badly. Then finally, he did the one thing that Whack Jack told him to never do. He went to the police and reported her as a missing person. When Whack Jack found out, he asked about it. Jacob said that he really cared about her. Then Whack Jack realized that he was actually telling the truth. Then he said, "Don't worry. I won't do anything, and I'll try everything on my end to find her." But he couldn't find her. He tried everything but nothing worked. Then Jacob cried himself to sleep at night. At that time, Jacob realized that he really cared about Olivia and he could not live without her. So, he decided to tell her how he really feels the moment he finds her again. But he was unable to find her.

Then after about a week, he got a phone call from an unknown number in the evening. At that time, he was at home thinking about Olivia. Then when he answered, it was one of his goons. He had found Olivia in a nearby crack house. Then Jacob quickly went there and when he saw her, she was high as fuck and was tripping. She saw him and said, "Heyyyyy." But that's it. She couldn't say anything more than that because she was that high. Then he carried her and put her in the car with the help of his goon. He brought her to his apartment and let her sleep it off until she got back to normal. She slept for almost 24 hours straight. Jacob never left her sight until she woke up because he didn't know where she would go if she woke up by herself.

When she woke up, she apologized to Jacob and said that she was ashamed of herself. Jacob asked, "Why did you do it? I mean everything was fine for you, right? Did I do anything wrong?"

She said, "Hell no Jacob. It's not your fault. It's mine. I found out that my grandma was dead. It was a very big deal for me because I grew up with her. So, I had to do something. The next thing I know, I was buying crack. I think I haven't eaten in days. Damn, I'm hungry. Do you have anything to eat?"

Jacob quickly gave her a burger because he knew that it was her favorite and she always liked to have a burger on their lunch outings. So, he already sent one of his bodyguards to get one before she woke up. Then she kissed him on the cheek and said, "You are my knight, sweety. I don't know what I would do without you."

She ate the whole burger in a minute. Jacob realized how hungry she was. She looked so weak but after the burger, she regained some energy. He felt sad for her but when she got up, he had his hopes up again. He tried to tell her how he really felt about her but she looked so tired so he decided to tell her that later.

Then he told her, "Well, You should get some sleep cuz you look like shit. I charged your phone and here it is. If you need anything, just call me okay. My guard will be outside all the time so don't worry. And please, make yourself at home. Mi casa su casa," then he winked.

She thanked him again and told him that she don't know how to repay what he did for her. He said no problem and went outside. Then he told his bodyguards to keep an eye on her. He went to see Whack Jack to tell him that he found Olivia. But before that, he went to the police to tell them that he found her.

In the evening, his bodyguard called him and told him that they have lost Olivia. They said that they went out to have a smoke for 10 minutes. After they came, the door was opened, and she has left Jacob's apartment. Jacob had no choice but to go back. When he tried to call her, she didn't answer. Then he sent her a message to call him back, but she didn't respond to it either. He went everywhere to look for her. He went to every crack house he knew but she was not in any of them. Then he gave up and went to his apartment. Then around 10 p.m. someone knocked on his door in a hurry. He quickly opened it and it was Olivia. Jacob was relieved and angry at the same time. He tried his best not to shout at her. He just looked at her with angry eyes, but she had no clue because she was high.

She went inside without an invitation and told him to close the door. Then she said, "Okay. Here is the thing. I want some crack cuz I'm losing my mind here."

Jacob said, "Hell no, Olivia. I'm not gonna give you crack. Look at yourself. You have lost your shit again."

She looked at him and walked towards him and said, "It's just a little crack, baby. Come on. I need it. I will do anything. I know you want to fuck me right. I'll let you fuck me till my pussy bleed."

He stopped her because he knew she didn't mean that and he wanted to have a good moment to tell her how he felt, not this half high bullshit moment of realization. So, he said, "It's more complicated than that okay."

Then she said, "I like you and you like me right." Jacob nodded yes because that was basically it. "Well, since we both like each other and each has something to give in return, why don't we do it."

"Do what Olivia?"

"You get me some crack. And I will let you fuck me with that foot-long dick."

She started to blink super-fast and started to touch her face like a crack head. Jacob knew that he had to give her something because being half high is worse than getting high to the fullest because she will go look for more if he doesn't give her anything. If he gave her some, then at least he will be there to control the amount. So, he said, "Okay. I will get you some crack, but I don't want to fuck you."

She nodded yes like a kid while smiling. Then he commanded her to sit and she quickly listened to him and sat on a chair. He called his guard and told him he needed some crack. After about 10 minutes, his guard came and gave him the crack. Olivia tried to jump in and take it, but Jacob said no and commanded her to sit again like a dog. She sat but she couldn't resist the temptation. Jacob knew that and that's why he wanted her to at least try to control herself. So, after she sat down, he said, "Okay. This is pure A grade crack, okay. You will not get over-dosed and you will get a super clear and clean high with this. But this is the first and the last time I'm going to give you crack, okay?"

She nodded and asked for a lighter and a spoon. She wanted to inject it into her bloodstream. It was the most dangerous and riskiest method of getting high, but people wanted to use that method because it was also the most effective and efficient way of getting high. Then Jacob said, "Hell no. you will not inject that shit in my house. You can snort it or smoke it. What do you prefer?"

Then she said she wants to snort it. So, Jacob smashed it until it was powdery and gave it to Olivia to snort. She snorted more than half of it at once. Then her body started to shake a lot. Then she screamed, "God damn. This is the best shit I have ever had." She slapped her head a couple of times and snorted the rest. Jacob didn't say a word when she snorted that crack. He just waited and let her do her thing.

Then after she finished, she came on to him and jump on him. Then she started to kiss him like a freak. He tried to stop her at first, but it felt too good to avoid so he kissed her back. He grabbed her by her ass and squeezed her ass cheeks. She was wearing just a t-shirt and shorts. She removed her shirt while Jacob was holding her, then she removed her bra also. She pushed her boobs against Jacob's face. He felt her boobs and they were so much smoother than he imagined. He started to suck her nipples. She had usually large nipples, but they were pink instead of brown. It felt like he was sucking on a flower. Then he carried her to the sofa and put her on it. Then he started to suck her nipples again. She told him to bite them, so he bit them firmly and she said, "Harder, daddy. I can't feel a thing." It was because she was high, and Jacob realized that. But he didn't want to disappoint her so he bit her nipples a bit harder. He also loved a little rough sex, so he didn't mind biting her nipples at all. Then she said, "Bite them till I say stop." He bit them, but she didn't say stop. He got afraid and stopped.

She got up and went to get her bag. From it, she took out two new injection needles. Then she said, "I want you to stick these on my nipples like piercings. Can you do that?" Then he said okay. He knew that she wouldn't feel pain since she was high. So, he took one needle and inserted it into her left nipple on the side. Then he continued till the needle came out the other side of the nipple. She moaned the whole time and it was out of pleasure and a little bit of pain. Now, the needle was attached to her nipple like a piercing. Then she said, "Now do the other nipple." He picked the second needle and inserted it into the right nipple like before. It didn't bleed even a little the first time, but it bled a bit when he inserted the second needle because she moaned a lot and moved a bit because she was super excited. Then she said, "Now lick them. Lick them hard."

He started to lick them. At first, he thought that it would hurt her, but she liked it. So, he started to lick them as hard as he could. He couldn't suck them since they had long needles, so he licked them and showered them with his saliva. Then he removed her shorts and her panty. She had a lot of pubes on her pussy. But she had trimmed them in the shape of a heart and it was so damn cute. He started to rub her pubs with his nose and mouth and then he started to lick her pussy. She started to moan. He slowly put a finger inside her pussy and started to move it in and out. Then she said, "I want to suck your dick first."

Then she stood up and removed his pants. She saw his foot-long dick for the first time. It was the biggest and the thickest dick she has ever seen. She was amazed by the size of it. She said, "My God, is this real?" It's like she lost a little bit of her high after seeing that humongous dick. Then she took her arm and put it next to his dick and started to measure it. At that time, Jacob had a huge erection, so his dick was bigger than Olivia's arm. Then she looked at his dick for a couple of seconds and started to suck it like a crazy person. But she could only suck a tiny bit of his huge dick. She was barely able to put it inside her mouth because it was so bigger than her mouth. Then she spat on it and showered it with saliva and rubbed it with both her hands. She started to jerk it off like a freak. It was clear that, that dick was too big for her. It was like she was fighting with an anaconda. But also, she was obsessed with that dick. She wanted all of it inside her.

Then she said, "Now put it inside my pussy." She sat on the side of the sofa because it was taller than where she was sitting. Then she put her legs up and opened her pussy with her fingers. She said, "Come to mama." It was so obvious to Jacob that his dick was so damn big for her tiny pussy. But it looked like she wanted it. Then he spat on her pussy and tried to insert his dick inside it. At first it was so tight. He was barely able to put the tip of his dick inside her pussy. Then she said, "Wait. I forgot something." She went and took her purse. Then she took another shorter needle. Then she gave it to Jacob and said, "Now stick this in my tongue."

She opened her mouth and put out her tongue. It became clear to Jacob that she needed the pain to have sexual feelings. He knew that he must do what she asked even though it's uncomfortable for him or she might not enjoy their sex. So, he pinned it on the middle of her tongue. It looked like a tongue piercing. Then she said "Squeeze it. I want to taste my blood". Then Jacob used two fingers to squeeze it, but he didn't squeeze it hard enough. Then she said, "Don't be a pussy and squeeze it." He got angry and embarrassed because no one had called him a pussy in a long time, especially a girl. So, he squeezed her tongue till it sprayed blood on his face. She screamed out of pain. He knew that it was too much for her, but he didn't apologize. Then he spat on her pussy again and inserted his dick in it. This time, he didn't think about whether it would hurt her or not. He thrust his dick into her pussy with all he had. It was too much for her pussy and her body. It was like an elephant trying to fuck a deer. She couldn't stay still while he was fucking her. So, he grabbed her by her waist and held her still. Up to this moment, he managed to put about 75% of his dick inside her pussy. It was actually the most, any woman was able to take in their pussy. So, this was a new feeling for Jacob. He finally was able to have a satisfying sexual experience. He decided to insert the rest of his dick also. So, he took her and put her down on the floor while his dick was inside her pussy. Then he jumped on to her body and held her legs up and forced his dick inside her pussy. She screamed with agony because it was too much for her, but Jacob couldn't stop. He finally managed to put his entire dick inside her pussy. It felt like he has reached climax even though he didn't because it was a whole new experience for him. He has never able to insert his entire dick inside a pussy until this moment. Then he looked at Olivia and she was enjoying it more than him. He got this new energy because of how Olivia was looking at him, so he started to fuck her so damn hard until she squirted all over the floor. It was like a fucking fire hose. She was not able to control herself. He took his dick out and she squirted everywhere. She screamed, cried and shook like a fish while squirting. It was obvious that she had reached the peaked level of sexual pleasure.

Then she touched her pussy and covered it with her hand. She waited for a couple of seconds. She swiped her face with her hands and held her legs up and looked at Jacob. She didn't say a word nor did Jacob. Then he inserted his dick inside her pussy again. This time, she didn't make too much noise because she was feeling too tired already. Jacob managed to put in his entire dick again because her pussy and everything around her was already wet by all the liquid she squirted. Then he leaned onto her and bit her chin while fucking her. He fucked her again and again and again until he almost reached climax. Then she screamed "stop" because she wanted to squirt again but Jacob didn't stop because he couldn't. He was so close to cumming, so he fucked her with everything he had until he came inside her. Then after he came, she stopped moving at all. He took his dick out of her pussy. She started to shake more than before and started to rub her pussy till it bled. She couldn't squirt a lot because her tank was already empty. This time, it was different because she was too weak, and she couldn't control herself. Then she stopped shaking and stopped moving at all. He looked at her with satisfaction because he knew that both of them enjoyed the sex to the fullest.

He said, "Damn girl. You are the only girl who managed to fuck my entire dick. You should be proud of yourself. For a little girl, you know how to handle a giant cock." Then he looked at her, but she didn't respond. He went near her to check on her, but she was not breathing. It's like she had a stroke. Then he quickly called 911 and started to give her CPR. He didn't know how to properly do that so he called his guards. They came inside and asked what happened because it looked like he has tortured her and raped her. Jacob couldn't think straight. Then David said, "Okay boss. You called 911 right? So, that means we have about 15 minutes to make this not look like a crime scene. James, go grab some clothes and clean her up and all this squirt. And boss, tell me how many needles you put on her." He said that he put two on her nipples and one in her tongue. Then he removed them slowly while James cleaned everything. Then he told Jacob to get him her clothes. Then he put them on her and picked her up and put her on the bed. Then he said, "Okay boss, this is what happened. She got overdosed, okay." Then Jacob nodded yes because otherwise he could go to jail for attempted murder and rape.

David continued, "Tell the cops that you found her like this. Where is the rest of the meth I got you?" Jacob took it from his pocket. David took it and put it inside her purse. Then after they cleaned everything, David asked, "Do you have the keys to her apartment?" Jacob said no. Then David checked her purse and found the key. They grabbed her body and took her to her apartment. Then they went away but Jacob decided to stay with her against David's advice. After the ambulance came, he told them that he found her like that, and he thinks that she overdosed. Then they quickly took her to the hospital. He stayed with her all the time, but she didn't respond. Then after everything, the doctors managed to save her. But she was in a coma. The doctor told Jacob that she had a sudden stroke. He said that it was so common for drug abusers and now, there is nothing to do but wait. Then he asked when she would wake up. Then the doctor said, "Well it could be days or weeks or maybe years. No one can tell it for sure. That's the messed-up thing about comas." It was so sad for him. He started to love her even more when they had sex but looked as if it was a one-time thing and he might lose her forever. He went home and slept.

The next day, he had to go to the police to give a statement. At first, he was afraid because he came inside her, but they didn't check anything in her pussy because it was obvious what caused the stroke. The blood test was positive for crack and there were extra needles in her purse. Luckily, the doctors didn't notice the needle marks on her nipples and tongue. So finally, Jacob was in the clear. He was relieved but he felt responsible for what happened to Olivia because he gave her the drugs and he was the one who literally fucked her brains out. So, he decided to go and check on her every day until she woke up. But sadly, she never woke up. He went to look for her for almost five years but then he found another girl and he couldn't tell her what happened between him and Olivia. So, he started to forget about her little by little. Then after about 10 years since her stroke, Jacob got a call from the hospital that she died because of lung failure. He got a little sad but at that time, he couldn't do anything, and he didn't feel responsible anymore. But he decided to give her a proper funeral since she had no other family. When he buried her, he remembered how he felt about her. Then a tear fell from his eye but that was it. It was just a flashback of how he felt love for the first time in his life. It was a life that was not meant to be.

THE END

03

The Brown Man On Heaven

Sanjay's home country was India. He lived there until his early 30s. He was happy at home when he was little. He had everything. He came from a middle-class family, so they didn't have a lot of money, but money was not a big issue for them. He was the eldest son in the family, and he had eight other siblings. There were only three boys in his family including him. All the rest were girls. The last two were boys. There was a huge age gap between him and his youngest brother. His youngest brother was born when Sanjay was 19 years old. So, it felt like he is more of a son than a brother to him.

His family lived in a village called Rajana in Mumbai. In this village, it is a tradition that women didn't work. It's the man's duty to provide for the family. People in this village and the whole area didn't believe in family planning. They said that it was a curse from God and they should overpopulate as much as they could. It was the dumb mindset the old generation had. Sanjay didn't believe in any of that but his mom and dad strongly believed it. That's why his parents had so many kids and it was the same story for most families. The society respected the parents based on the number of kids they had. So, everyone wanted to have as many kids as possible. They didn't think about the consequences of having lots of kids. Some families even had more than 15 kids to the same parents. The kids would suffer a lot when the parents couldn't provide for the family. So, they would die young or suffer for most of their childhood. There were no child protective services, so the kids were hopeless. It was a living hell for kids in Rajana. So, for boys, it became a must to work as soon as they turned 18. It was worse for families that didn't have male kids. Sometimes, the father couldn't provide for the family and yet they would refuse to use protection when having sex. So, they would reproduce again and again until the whole family collapsed. It was so common in Rajana. When that happened, others would say that the parents were bad people and that's why God didn't bless them or some shit like that. Or they would say that the newborn was a cursed child and that's why the whole family collapsed.

There were a lot of ways for families to collapse because of their beliefs. Mostly, the father would sacrifice everything he has to the temple in order to get some treasure from God. So, when that doesn't work out, the father would think that he is the curse and kill himself. Then the mother and the kids would have nothing. It was so common than anyone would think. In these cases, if the family had at least one grown male child, then they would still have hope. Otherwise, the family will have nothing; not even a roof over their head because the roof they had would have been sacrificed by the father. It was the foolish mindset the society had.

It became harder and harder for Sanjay's family when his parents wouldn't stop making children. He was the only male kid in the family until his younger brothers were born. After him, there were five sisters and in their society, females are considered useless because they can't work for money. So, until they get married, they are only a huge burden to the family. Sanjay didn't have any choice but to get a job the day he turned 18 because his father could barely provide. So, at first, he worked as a librarian in the town library. He didn't like that job even a little bit, but he had no other choice. But he had lots of access to books because of his new job role. So, he studied everything he could get his hands on when he had time. Then finally, he found his passion. It was computer programming. His English was not that good but for some reason, he could understand programming like his mother tongue. It's like he could understand computers better than humans. He knew that programming is what he had to do for the rest of his life. But the issue was, he didn't have any qualifications in the subject area. He must have at least a diploma in computer programming to get a job. At that time in India, programming was not a popular field and one must have access to a computer to learn it properly, which is something Sanjay didn't possess. He hadn't even seen a computer. He learned everything through books. He knew that programming would be an essential subject to the world, but he knew that he would have to wait until that happens because he had no money to study for a diploma or buy a computer. So, he studied everything about computers and programming languages through books. He even studied things about robotics. He had a lot of knowledge, but he had no way of proving it. Then finally, when he was about to become 25, they finally got a computer in their library. It was the happiest day of his life. No one knew how to operate it except for Sanjay. Even though he didn't have practical knowledge, he had all the necessary theoretical knowledge on how to operate a computer. He already knew everything about software and hardware from inside out. Therefore, the library put him in charge of the computer. Everyone came to him to get things done from the computer. Consequently, he spent most of his time with it. He forgot all his problems when he was with the computer. He got obsessed with it. He learned everything through that computer. He had an internet connection also, but it was so slow at the beginning. Then he managed to file an inquiry and get a better connection. He stated that he needed a faster internet connection to operate things in the library. He then made a database using MySQL without anyone's help.

Then that news spread through the tech community in his area really fast. There were not much of tech geniuses in his area. So, his work got highlighted with ease. Then he got a scholarship from the head of his local university. He managed to go to that university from his home and because it was so close to his library, he managed to continue his work in the library on the weekend as a part-time librarian. He was busy all the time. He had lectures all day every weekday. Thus, he had no time to learn extra things on weekdays. He started to go to the library early in the morning. He had lots of work, but he liked it because he had to do everything through a computer. He started to write new programs to make his work easier. He became so good at it and word got around the campus that he was a genuine tech genius. He managed to finish his diploma in two years. He got lots of job offers to be a software engineer more than anyone because of the things he did while studying. His academic advisor encouraged Sanjay to finish the degree before going to a full-time job, but he had to go to get a job because the situation in his house had gotten worse; his father got sick and couldn't work. So, the whole family had to rely on him. He took the offer that paid the most. The money was good. He could easily provide for his family with that salary. So, everything got better.

He didn't have any kind of social life. Even in the university, he had no friends. He studied by himself and did projects by himself. He had a couple of group projects. Even in those, he only communicated with them only when he had to. He avoided human contact as much as possible. Even in the library, he worked alone. He avoided everyone so he had no real friends or any friends. He only had fellow colleagues and fellow undergraduates. He didn't even talk a lot with his lecturers. He didn't talk with his siblings also. He just went home and did things by himself. Sanjay didn't even talk with his parents much. But they knew that it was how he was and he was not just being rude. His mom loved him so much and told him that he was special, and he was destined to do great things. She always said that the meaning of the word Sanjay is victory and it was given by Lord Shiva. He never believed any of that stuff, but he cared about his family and especially his mom. So, he didn't tell her how he felt about stuff that she believed in because he knew that it would break her heart to pieces.

Sanjay's father died when Sanjay was in his early 30s. He had a lung failure and doctors recommended to do surgery but his father refused. Instead, he went to the temple and vowed to God and said that he would donate food to the poor if he was cured. Sanjay tried his best to take his father to take those tests and get the proper treatments, but he refused because of his dumb beliefs. So, as Sanjay predicted, his father faced a painful and meaningless death. Sanjay got so angry with his father after he died because later, he found out that what his father had was completely curable with modern technology and treatments. That's when he told his mom what he thought of her religion and her stupid beliefs. He said that he never wants to be a part of a family that believes that stupid stuff. He said that he will not provide for his family anymore if his mom tried to teach the rest of his siblings her stupid beliefs and religion because most of his sisters already were huge followers and believers of it. Sanjay told his mom that his dad would still be alive today if it weren't for his stupid beliefs. He said that their religion is the reason that his father is dead. At first, she didn't believe it and said that it was just a curse that God has fallen upon them. But later Sanjay managed to convince his mom that her beliefs are completely false, and they shouldn't rely on them even a little. Then he managed to convince his mom to convince his sisters of the falseness of her beliefs.

After that, Sanjay decided to move to Italy. He got a huge job offer from a robotic company and it was actually his dream job. He loved programming but he loved to program robots even more. He decided to send his mom a quarter of his salary. It was more than enough for his family to have everything they needed. At first, he thought of sending them half of his salary, but he knew that his mom would definitely waste the extra cash on stupid religious items. Also, since he had six sisters, he had to save money for each of their dowry. It was compulsory in his village. Otherwise, no man would marry any of his sisters. So, he needed all the cash he could save. Therefore, he decided to save as much as possible after moving to Italy.

He moved to Italy when he was 32 years old. At first, it was so hard for him because his English was not that good, and he knew nothing about Italy. But he loved working on his new company. He became a tech lead in his company within 2 years and it was a pretty big deal. His initial salary doubled after his latest promotion, but he didn't increase the amount he sent home because he had to save so much for his sisters. He didn't change one bit after he came to Italy. He was the same as before. He had zero human contact. He had to interact with people a lot after his latest promotion but even so, he tried his best to do those things through emails or messages or chats. He was a genius at that too. He genuinely managed to avoid most of the compulsory human interactions using those things without anyone noticing. He was so cunning at that. Also, because of that, he became so damn good at chatting. He never had a girlfriend in his life or any real friend. So, he was so awkward in social gatherings. He knew that but he also knew that no one would be better than him when it came to social media chatting. He had a fake Facebook profile and he stalked a lot of his colleagues on it. He managed to get most of the prettiest girls in his office to fall for him using his fake account. Most girls would send him nudes and asks for dick pics in return. He always sends his own dick pics and then, they would want to meet him. But when that happens, he always finds an excuse not to meet them because he was too shy.

Sanjay was an average looking guy. There was nothing attractive about him, but he was not ugly either. He was 5 feet and 7 inches tall. He had normal wavy hair and a normal looking beard. He was a little fat, but it was not that big of a deal. His dick was average size, but he was ashamed of it. He thought that it was not long enough to please a woman. His fake Facebook profile had a picture of an uglier man than him. Thus, he knew that the reason for him to get all those girls was his chatting skills. He was so proud of that skill, but he could never get any girl because online chatting was the only thing he was good at. He even avoided video calls and even normal calls. He had this phobia toward women, especially toward pretty ones. He had a lot of young beautiful developers working under him. He could have easily had sex with them because of his status but he couldn't because he was socially awkward. His boss knew about his social awkwardness. At first, it was not a problem for his boss because Sanjay only did programming stuff. But when he got his promotions and had a higher status among the company, it became a big issue for his boss. So, he recommended a therapist for Sanjay.

At first, he didn't like to see the therapist because it involved talking and human interaction. But after a couple of sessions, he got so comfortable with his therapist because he was so good at his job and managed to get Sanjay's attention. Then Sanjay talked with him about everything. The therapist said that his social phobias are not that uncommon, but he must address them, or it will get worse. Then he suggested dating. But it was a huge step for him. Because of the therapist, Sanjay also got close with his boss. His name was Giovanni and he was a playboy. Even though he was in his early 50s, no one could assume his age. He was divorced twice and had four kids. He always kept his personal life and his professional life separately. No one in his company has ever seen his kids or his ex-wives. His kids lived with his ex-wives and he just paid child support. He really liked Sanjay. He knew that Sanjay was a tech genius. Giovanni was more of a management guy. He knew lots of things about technologies, but he was not good at all at programming and engineering. But he was the best at talking to people. He was a word genius. He could convince almost anyone on almost anything after talking with them for a while. He knew that and it was his most valuable skill. He never hesitated to abuse that skill. It was the only skill he had and needed to climb up the corporate ladder. He managed to keep everyone on his good side. He had no enemies and he never tried to abuse his status to get what he wanted. He had his conversational skills for that and his looks. He had a muscular body and all women in the company craved a piece of him. So, his status was just a plus for him. He was so rich, but he never went to strip clubs or fucked prostitutes because he didn't have to. He got all the sex he wanted because of his looks and flirting skills.

He was really worried about Sanjay because he had no social life. Giovanni was Sanjay's mentor. So, he knew everything about him. Giovanni knew his past, what happened with his family, how much he hated his parent's beliefs and why he saves money as much as he could. He tried to change him for all those years, but he couldn't. It's like Sanjay was meant to be alone by himself. Then one day, Sanjay got caught by one of his fellow female colleagues when he was sexting with her through his fake Facebook account. Her name was Sarah and at that time, she was in love with him because of his texting skills. He sexted with her a lot and through that, he managed to make her cum a lot of times. She even admitted that she never had any sexual pleasures that strong when she had real sex. So, she really wanted to meet him but as usual, Sanjay avoided that.

The way he got caught was actually pretty fucked up. Sanjay usually goes to his fake profile through his laptop. He always had two laptops open because of his workload and it was convenient for him. Sarah was a team leader. She had her own team and her own project. Sanjay was her boss at the time and that means she had to report to him directly. He always used texting and email to communicate with her so he could avoid talking with her face to face. But sometimes, Sanjay had to do group meetings with the whole team. Usually, he had to go to them to do this, but he never did. He always used conference video calls to have the meeting with the whole team.

One day, Sarah requested a meeting with him, but he was at home that day because he was on sick leave. Then he agreed and they would do a conference video call. He set up his laptop in his room and began the video call with the team. He didn't talk much as usual, so Sarah did most of the talking. But halfway through the call, she saw that in Sanjay's background he had his second laptop and the screen was visible for all and on that screen, Sanjay's fake profile was showing. He forgot to close his laptop before starting the conference call. Then she realized that it was a familiar profile, but she couldn't identify it right away. So, she took a couple of screenshots of the video call so she could analyze them later. Then after the call ended, she zoomed those pictures and realized that it was the profile of the person she is in love with. When she zoomed more, she saw her chat with him on the side of it. She didn't have to double check that chat with her chat because he sent her a message right before the conference call. She got so furious and heartbroken at the same time. She could never think of Sanjay like that. She had the utmost respect for him for his knowledge, but she never thought of him in a sexual way and she never thought that a socially awkward person like that could be that good at online flirting. She was the prettiest girl in the company and every man wanted her, but she had such high standards. Then she finally fell for a person that didn't even exist. She got depressed that day because she never felt sorrow like that in her life. Therefore, she had no choice but to tell that to Sanjay's boss. She went to see him and told him everything. At that time, Sanjay knew nothing.

Giovanni couldn't believe what Sarah was saying because he never suspected Sanjay to be that good. She then showed him the whole chat and the screenshots of the conference call. Then Giovanni told her to not tell anyone about this and told her to take a week off. Also, he said that he would handle it. When he sent Sarah home, he made her block Sanjay's fake profile from her account before she left. Then Giovanni started to think. It was like he has found a treasure. He always liked to help people get laid. It was his hobby. He was genuinely worried about Sanjay and thought that he was a lost cause. But with this, he knew that there was still hope for Sanjay. So, he sent a message from him to come and see him first thing in the morning.

When Sanjay went to see him in the morning, he didn't have a clue about what happened to Sarah. He thought that the reason that she blocked him on Facebook was because she got mad about something. So, he didn't think much about that. Then he went and Giovanni offered him a seat and asked if he wanted anything to drink. Sanjay said no and then Giovanni started to speak, "Ok Sanjay, you have done something very bad." Then he looked straight into Sanjay's eyes, but he didn't say anything. Giovanni wanted to stare at him until he said something because he knew otherwise Sanjay won't say a word.

Then Sanjay slowly asked, "What was it?"

Giovanni said, "Well, I'm glad that you asked. Do you know that you can't have an affair with a fellow colleague unless you have cleared that with human resources?" Then Sanjay nodded yes. But Giovanni wanted him to speak so he asked the same question again. Then Sanjay said yes. Giovanni continued, "Well, that applies to you also."

Sanjay was now confused because he didn't have an affair with anyone in his company. Then Giovanni said, "I know about Sarah. What you did to her was fucked up man. She knows it's you."

Then Sanjay's heart started to beat so fast. He got afraid because he has never gotten caught like that before. This was a whole new experience for him and he started to have a panic attack. He tried to speak up, but he couldn't. Giovanni saw how scared Sanjay was, but he wanted to dominate him and make him kneel to him mentally. So, he said, "I told her that I would take care of this. I gave her a week off from work but that won't be enough. She gave me the whole chat between the two of you. It's like you have become so intimate with her."

Sanjay had nothing to do but smile at him. Then he slowly said, "She started it."

Then Giovanni laughed and said, "Man, do you think that a girl like that would ever start a conversation with a normal guy like that in your fake profile? Don't bullshit a bullshitter, okay? I know that you managed to make her feel everything with only texts. I mean you managed to make her pussy wet with your thumbs and that was impressive even for me man. I mean what the fuck. You are a genius." He started to laugh.

Sanjay was confused because a second ago, Giovanni was mad at him for breaking Sarah's heart but now he's impressed by his skill. Then Giovanni said, "Come on man. You are smooth like a freaking butterfly. I mean, I know I am a smooth talker but damn, you took it to a whole new level. I couldn't believe that man. I read your whole chat last night. How did you come up with that stuff?" Sanjay smiled when he said that because he didn't know how to respond. Instead, he became embarrassed. Then Giovanni said, "Come on man, if you can text like that, you can talk like that. That's a fact. I mean damn man. I know players in the texting field, but you are the champion." Then he poured a glass of whiskey for them both. He insisted that Sanjay drink with him. Giovanni cheered for Sanjay's new-found skill.

Then Sanjay said, "So what's next?" He waited a long time to ask that because he didn't want to disturb Giovanni's excitement.

"What's next? Buddy we gotta get you laid ASAP. Otherwise, what's the point of being so damn smooth?"

"Oh no, I'm fine with what I have."

"Bullshit, your therapist said everything about you."

Then Sanjay got furious because he truly trusted his therapist and he had betrayed that trust completely.

Giovanni said, "Don't worry bro. It's not his fault. He is a good friend of mine. I just asked him about you when he was super drunk. He probably doesn't remember saying that. So, no worries." Then he patted Sanjay on the back and said, "I know you are a virgin." From the reaction from Sanjay's face when he said that, he realized that it was completely true because the reaction was that obvious. Then Giovanni said, "You have everything bro. You have money and an awesome job. And I know that you are not gay because no gay man can text with a girl like that. So, why the fuck are you living as a virgin?"

Sanjay had no choice but to tell him the truth. He said, "I'm awkward, okay. You know how uncomfortable I get around people, especially around pretty girls. Take Sarah for example. I texted her till she got wet, but I still can't look directly in her eyes and say hi."

"Well, we can do something about that. What do you say?"

"What can we do about it?"

"Come to the club with me tonight. It's Friday so it will be a happening night. I'm not forcing you. I know that this is hard for you. But until you get out of your comfort zone, you cannot survive. You don't have to do anything. I will invite some of my friends. We will go out and have a couple of drinks. Sounds good?" Then Sanjay agreed to him because of two reasons. The first and the main reason was because he respected Giovanni a lot and he knew that what Giovanni said was right and he must go out and socialize more often. The second reason was he was actually afraid of what Giovanni would do with the information he had about him and Sarah. He thought that if he didn't agree to go out for drinks with him, he would use them to hurt his reputation. So, from Sanjay's perspective, he had every reason to go because he had nothing to lose but a lot to gain.

After Sanjay went home, he quickly had a shower and trimmed his beard and shaved his armpits. He took out the best shirt he had and polished his shoes and ironed the outfit. It was the first time he cared about his looks for a long time. The last time he did that was when he got his latest interview for a promotion and it was about two years ago. So, he finally got ready and called an Uber because he didn't have a drivers' license. Then he went to the club on time. Giovanni said 7 p.m., so Sanjay came around 6.55 p.m. because he strongly believed in punctuality. But no one was there. So, he sent a message to Giovanni and he called Sanjay right back and said, "Damn man. No one would come to these things on time. Wait there. I'll be there as soon as I can, okay? Don't leave."

Giovanna arrived around 7.20 p.m. and they waited another 15 minutes until his friends arrived. Giovanni had a smoke while they waited. It was the first time Sanjay saw him smoke because he has never done that in the office. Then after his friends arrived, they went inside. It was a posh club and there was a huge line. But the bouncer knew Giovanni and the rest, so he let them in, but they stopped Sanjay and Giovanni said, "Don't worry. He's with us." It was then the bouncer let him inside. Sanjay felt special when that happened because he saw the look on everyone's faces that were in the line. Even the girls were impressed because he managed to get inside without being in a queue. It gave him a sudden confidence and he liked that feeling because that was something he has never felt before.

It was so loud inside the club. Everyone was either dancing or drinking or both. Some people were doing drugs out in the open and some were smoking weed. The whole club was covered in smoke and it was somewhat irritating for Sanjay because he hated the smell of cigarettes. But he tried his best to keep a straight face because he really wanted to see this through. Then they went to the backstage of the DJ. It was a restricted area, so no one was there. Then they went upstairs from there and there was a sign that said, "VIP ONLY" and Giovanni and the rest went there like it was not a big deal, but Sanjay froze because no one else was there. Everyone was on the lower floor. Then Giovanni said, "Don't worry brother. We are very important people. This area is allocated for us. So come," then he winked. So, Sanjay followed him inside to the VIP area. It was so different than the rest of the club. It was completely soundproof so they would not hear any sound from the outside but they could see everything because there was a huge glass wall between them and the DJ. The VIP lounge was a huge balcony and it was covered with that glass wall so everyone inside it could see the dance floor.

Then a very beautiful waitress came, and Giovanni said, "Bring each of us shots every 10 minutes until one of us passes out." He gave the girl a hefty tip and slapped her ass as she went with their order. It was like he was swarming in confidence. To Sanjay, how Giovanni acted there was so unique. He never thought that he could act like Giovanni ever. Then they got vodka shots and everyone drank them with ease. Then Giovanni said, "Okay, guys, this is a good friend of mine Sanjay." Everyone introduced themselves to Sanjay. It turns out that everyone was rich like Giovanni but none of them looked like him. They were all the same age range, but everyone else's age was shown. They were fat and had gray hair. Most of them had dad bodies and everyone was married with kids.

Then Sanjay slowly asked Giovanni, "Are your friends all people older than you?" He managed to ask that without anyone hearing because Sanjay was sitting next to Giovanni.

Giovanni laughed and said, "No brother. We all are the same age. These are friends I have known for a long time. But the main reason I go out with them is because they look old. You know what I'm saying. Next to them, I look young and awesome. They don't realize it, but they are the best wingmen I could ever ask for. I will always get the best girl when I'm with them. While they use their money to get a girl, I use my looks and skills to do the same even when I'm far richer than these fuckers." Then he laughed again. It made total sense. Even the pretty waitress showed some affection toward him and only him. When the others tried to talk with her, she avoided them and only tried to talk with Giovanni. It was so smart on Giovanni's part because it really worked. Then Giovanni asked Sanjay, "Are you willing to spend 1,000 euros to get laid tonight?" Sanjay said yes because he knew that he would not get a chance like this again and also 1,000 euros was not that much of a deal for him if he had a good chance of getting laid for the first time in his life. Then Giovanni told the waitress to send a couple of drinks to the next table and told her to tell them that the drinks were from Sanjay. There were only a couple of young hot girls in that table.

Sanjay didn't understand at first what Giovanni was planning to do but he trusted him because he knew that Giovanni was a pretty smart guy. Then after the waitress sent the other table the drinks, she pointed to Sanjay and told them something. Giovanni signaled them to come to their table and they came. There were five girls in that table but only four guys on Sanjay's table including him. Then after they came, Giovanni introduced everyone to them, and he realized that one girl was particularly interested in Sanjay. So, he quickly told that girl about Sanjay and introduced him again to her and smoothly made her sit next to him. Then two girls sat next to Giovanni and the rest sat with the other two friends of Giovanni. They started to talk. Giovanni signaled Sanjay to relax because at first, he was so damn nervous. But after a couple of shots, he got a huge confidence boost not because of the shots but because of the environment. He felt safe there and he knew that this girl was really interested in him. He knew that he was not talking to a girl through a fake profile. He realized that he is really talking with a pretty girl. Maybe she is interested in him only for his money, but he didn't care one bit. He understood that he has a real chance of getting laid with this girl because of all the signs she shows. She touched his knees a couple of times and that made his dick hard in seconds. So, he touched her knees and she didn't resist. She wanted him to do more.

Also, having Giovanni next to him gave him a confidence boost. Then after about an hour, Giovanni said, "Shall we take this party somewhere else?" All the girls cheered when he said that. Sanjay didn't understand what was going to happen but he followed along. Then Giovanni called the waitress and told her to bring the bill. After he got it, he signaled Sanjay to pay it. It was because then the girls would realize that Sanjay is actually rich. Giovanni wanted to prove that without bragging about it. That's why he asked Sanjay if he is willing to spend some money that day. The bill was around one thousand euros. Sanjay thought that it was too expensive because they didn't have much but it was expensive because they were in the VIP lounge and the girls drank a lot of shots and their previous bill was also added to this bill. He had no choice but to pay it, but he was fine with it because he really wanted to impress the girl that was with him. After he paid the bill, Giovanni said, "You see that ladies, that's how my brother here spends for the good stuff. He is not just rich, he has a pretty good taste for high-quality stuff. So, it goes without saying, that you girls are also high-quality babes cuz Sanjay here chose you guys." After he said that, everyone laughed, and he winked at Sanjay. Then they got into three taxis and went to Giovanni's house.

There was no one there when they went there. Giovanni put on some music and took a Chivas Regal bottle and poured shots for everyone. Then while the girls were dancing, he pulled Sanjay out to a corner and said, "OK buddy. This is the time to shine. I brought the girls here because you couldn't fuck them at the club. But here, you have all the space and peace. Use any room you want upstairs. Just wait till she gets a little drunk. Have some drinks for yourself also and fuck that girl till your dick gets sore, okay?" Then he hugged Sanjay and wished him luck.

Sanjay knew it was now or never. So, he drank two more shots and waited until the girl got drunk. Then he went to her and said, "Shall we go somewhere private?" She agreed and he took her to a room upstairs. Then after she went inside, Sanjay locked the door. The door had an unusual lock, so it took a couple of seconds for him to lock it properly. After he locked the door, he turned around. There she was, completely naked. She had no clothes on her. She managed to remove every piece of clothing she had on her within seconds. Sanjay froze, and she came on to him and started to kiss him. It was his first kiss and the first time he has ever seen a girl naked for real. He got nervous but she did everything. She removed his pants and started to suck his dick. After it became super hard, she went and took a condom from her purse and put it on his dick. Then she bent over on the bed and said, "Now fuck me." Sanjay didn't know what came over him but he slowly went to her and he put his dick inside her pussy. At first, it was difficult but after a couple of seconds, he got the hang of it. So, he held her from her waist and started to fuck her like a pro. She started to moan and said, "Fuck me harder, baby." He knew that she was enjoying it so that gave him more motivation because he had this huge doubt about his dick, that it was not long enough to please a woman but now, he knew that he was wrong. So, he fucked her like that for a couple of minutes till he climaxed.

She looked at him with a satisfied face and said, "You are a late cummer, huh?"

He didn't quite get it because he thought that he climaxed quickly. Then he asked if she came too. Then she said, "Yeah baby. I came twice." She winked and started to get dress. Sanjay was so damn happy. He pulled up his pants and helped her get dress. Then she said, "Wow, what a gentleman."

He smiled and asked for her number and she said, "You are new to this aren't you baby. Don't get this wrong but this is just a one-night stand baby." She went downstairs and there was no one. It looked like everyone was busy by themselves like Sanjay was a couple of minutes ago. She then called a cab and went home. Sanjay took another couple of whiskey shots and went to that room where he had sex for the first time and slept because he didn't want to go home and also wanted to feel the room and live what he experienced again.

Then the next morning, he woke up around 7 a.m. When he went downstairs, he saw Giovanni and the two girls that were with him. It was obvious that he had a threesome with those girls. The rest of his friends left during the night. Then he said good morning to Sanjay and invited him to have breakfast with them. He had prepared an awesome breakfast for the two girls he had sex with and there was plenty more so

Sanjay stayed to have some. Then after they finished, the girls went away.

Giovanni asked, "So, you fucked her right. I can see from that smile." Then he high fived Sanjay who told him everything that happened. He said that he now has this weird confidence and now he is not afraid. He also asked Giovanni if he can go out with him and his gang more. Then Giovanni said, "Hell yeah brother. You are now in the gang. Once you are in, it's for life." Sanjay was happy and thanked him and said that he owes him for everything that he has done for him and he went home.

Sanjay went out with Giovanni and his friends every Friday after that. They had a couple of usual clubs but none of them were strip clubs. They had this rule. They would not have sex with prostitutes. They wanted to work on getting a girl. It was the satisfaction they craved, not just the sex. It was the same with Sanjay. He also wanted to sharpen his conversational skills with pretty women instead of just fucking them. After a month, Sarah left the company and before she quit, she told Sanjay to go to hell because she really has loved his fake profile and it was messed up for her to love someone that wasn't even real.

Sanjay got pretty good at talking to girls and getting laid. His social awkwardness began to fade away and this brought a new shining light to his life. His life has become a heaven for him. Things have finally begun to work for him, and he never forgot that all of this was because of Giovanni. Giovanni has become his new best friend. Even though he was technically his boss, but he didn't hesitate to ask him about anything both work-related or personal.

Then after a couple of months, he began to get bored with normal sex. He told that to his therapist. At first, he was not fine with his therapist because he had told Giovanni everything about him. But then he realized that it was because of that fact that Giovanni was able to help him so he thought that it was God's weird way of looking after him. Therefore, he had no problem with seeing the same therapist. He told him about his sexual desires. He said that even though he enjoys normal sex, he wanted more.

Then the therapist asked him, "Do you want to experience sexual relations with a male?"

Sanjay said "Oh no. I'm not gay. It's just that the sex is very predictable you know. First, you flirt, then you go somewhere private. Then you start to kiss and remove each other's clothes. Then we might do some oral sex and then usual sex and that's it. It's always that order. There is nothing more. I like to try anal sex but there is no way I can do that with this usual sex process you know. What should I do about that?"

Then his therapist said, "Well, I know what you mean. It's a very common thing among almost all of us. We all have different sexual desires. Some can say that we have different fetishes, and that's true. You just have to find a partner who is into some of the same fetishes you have. Now, it might be tricky because it's not an easy task. First, you have to find someone with the same interests. And then, you must be able to convince them to experience the same fetishes with you intimately."

Sanjay started to think of a way to do that. It was not easy. He tried to do that when he went to clubs with Giovanni, but he never could realize what the girl wants until he starts to have sex with them. Most of the time, the girl would be so drunk, so the sex would only last for about a couple of minutes. There would be not much foreplay. Therefore, he had no way of knowing for sure.

He thought about a way and then he got a virtual reality system. In it, there were some porn games with lots of categories. Hardcore sex and BDSM were top categories. Then he managed to get some satisfaction through it, but he wanted the real experience. So, he finally decided to tell Giovanni who suggested, "So, try Tinder or something." He said that like it was not that big of a deal.

Sanjay didn't understand him at first. So, when he asked about it, Giovanni said, "Well, use a dating app. In it, chicks usually post the kind of shit that they are into. You know, weird stuff like what you want. Make an account, find a girl with similar crap and swipe right or something. You are a pro in texting right? I don't think it would be hard for you since you know how to handle a pussy now." Then he laughed.

Sanjay did some research and realized that what Giovanni was saying was totally true. He realized that he should have gone to Giovanni at the beginning, but he was satisfied he found a way at least now.

So first, he made a Grindr account. He didn't realize that it was a dating app targeted for gays and transgender people. So, he had to make another account on Tinder. He tried to find a girl with similar interests, and he found a couple of girls. But the thing was they also had to swipe right for him in order for him to start a conversation with them. So, he had to wait until a girl with hardcore fetishes swiped right for him. After about a week and a half, a girl named Elena swiped right. She was only a couple of miles away. So, he managed to start a conversation with her. He used a unique pick up line. He texted, "Do you believe in love at first swipe?" Then she sent, "LOL. You are funny." Then he managed to get a date after chatting with her for a couple of days. It was a dinner date.

Instead of his usual clubs, he chose a fancy restaurant because he wanted to have sex while not being so drunk. There were only two photos in her Tinder profile and she refused to give him any details about her. So, he wasn't sure if he was being catfished.

But then she came. She was more gorgeous than in her profile pictures. She was about his height and she had blond hair up to her waist. It was curly hair, but it was shining like a light. She had large breasts and her ass was so perfect, he could eat it right then and there. She possessed a curvy body but it was so damn sexy. She had wide shoulders and her dress made them pop up even more. She was wearing a red frock and was wearing matching lipstick. She didn't have much makeup on her face. Some minor foundation and a little bit of eyeliner was all there was. Her dress was sleeveless and it was long, down to her knees. It was so obvious that her whole body was completely waxed. So, Sanjay thought that maybe her pussy was also waxed completely.

When she arrived at the table, he stood up as a gesture of respect. She came up to him and hugged him. Then he offered her a seat and then they started to speak. When the waiter said that they could order dinner, Elena said, "First we will have a couple of drinks." They got a wine bottle and they talked until it was finished. She told him that she was a tattoo artist. Then he said, "But you don't have any tattoos." Then she said, "I like my body as it is," and winked. Sanjay knew that the plan was in motion. She said that they should order dinner and she started to eat fast. Sanjay didn't want to startle her so he tried to have his dinner as fast as he could. After they finished, she said, "We should go somewhere private. I wanna have sex with you a lot."

Sanjay smiled and nodded yes like an idiot. Then he called an Uber and told the driver to take them to his house. Sanjay already cleaned his house because he was planning on taking Elena there. But then Elena said, "Well, I have to stop at my house for a second. Can we go there first?" He nodded yes and they went to her house. It was a small house and she was living a couple of blocks away from Sanjay's but he has never seen her in his life. She went in and came with a huge bag. So, he asked, "What's in it sweety." She said that it was a surprise. Then he spoke about the fact that she is living nearby but he has never seen her. She said that she moved there very recently. Finally, they came to Sanjay's house. After they went inside, Elena asked where the washroom was. Then she went there and told Sanjay to get ready. He already had a pack of condoms in his room. So, he went there and took them out while Elena was in the shower. After that, he poured glasses of whiskey for him and Elena.

As he poured them, she came outside. She was wearing a tiny black leather suit that barely covered her nipples and her pussy. It was so damn sexy. He saw that her pussy was waxed completely because most of her pussy was visible There was a zipper on the get up on top of her pussy and asshole. So, he knew that he doesn't have to remove it to fuck her. Then she took the whiskey glass and poured it on her chest and told him to lick it. Sanjay liked the sound of it, so he licked her cleavage but when he tried to touch her boobs, she hit him with a stick she had in her surprise bag. When he tried to suck her nipple, she hit him in his face and said, "Do what you are told, bitch." This caused Sanjay pain. Not just the hitting but also the fact that a girl calling him a bitch, but at the same time he found it arousing. Then she said, "Now drink that whiskey but don't swallow it. Then open my zipper and shoot that whiskey into my pussy and make it wet with whiskey." He knew that it would burn her pussy but that was exactly the kind of stuff he wanted to experience. Then he poured the whiskey to his mouth and opened her zipper while she was standing. Then he put his mouth on top of her pussy and shoots the whiskey as hard as he could inside her pussy. She screamed when he did that. He looked at her face while kneeling and she said, "Who told you to stop, huh? Now lick my pussy till I cum."

Then he realized that pain would only make her horny. So, he started to suck the top of her pussy while inserting three fingers at once into her pussy. It was already wet with all the whiskey, so it went right it with ease. Then he started to suck her clit so hard, she started to squirt a bit. Then she said, "God damn. You do know how to pleasure a woman. Okay, now go and take anything from that bag and insert it into my pussy." He went and looked at that bag. There were a lot of things and some of them were obviously so big to insert into her vagina. Then he looked at her while holding the bag and she said, "I said anything." There were a lot of dildos and some whips. One whip had a metal ending with sharp nails. So, he took it and the biggest dildo in the bag. It was purple and as big as his arm and was full of veins. At the side of it, it said "Dick of Thanos." He got happy with it because Sanjay was a huge Marvel fan. Then Elena had an impressed face and said "not bad" then she went and sat on a sofa in the living room.

She lay down on it and held her legs up and opened her pussy with her fingers. Then she told him, "Surprise me." At first, Sanjay thought that maybe he should use some lubricant to apply on that huge dildo. But since Elena told him to surprise her, he decided to do something else. He took the whiskey bottle and poured some of it all over on that dildo. Elena looked at that with a happy face and said, "Wow. I like how you think, babe." Then he started to insert it inside her pussy. She started to moan a lot at first but when he managed to insert it about two inches, she started to scream because it was so thick, and it burned her pussy because of the whiskey.

The dildo was about 12 inches long and he managed to insert almost 10 inches. Then she said, "Now fuck me in the ass while it's still in there." She was talking about the dildo. She wanted to keep it inside her pussy. Then he spat on her asshole and started to lick it. He really wanted to do that because no woman has ever let him do that because they were too shy or thought that their ass would smell bad. But with Elena, it was different. There were no limits. So, he ate her ass as much as he wanted. Then he took that whip and whipped her ass cheeks with it a couple of times while she was laying on the sofa. He held her legs with his left arm and whipped her ass under her legs with his right arm. The whip managed to welt her ass cheeks and made her bleed a lot. He only whipped her four times, but the other point had a lot of pointy edges like nails and it was metal. She wanted more but Sanjay knew that it wouldn't be wise to whip her more on the ass. So, he picked her up and made her stand. Then he turned her around and made her bend over on the sofa. Then he started to whip her back. He did it slowly at first so it would not make her bleed, but he knew that it was hurting enough because the whip actually looked like it was used for genuine torture. Then he spat on her asshole and inserted his dick inside it again. It has become tight again but then she spread her ass cheeks with her hands so he could insert it. Then he managed to insert his entire dick. His stomach and waist touched her ass while he fucked her and because of that, his waist and the lower stomach were covered in blood. It was like gore sex, but he enjoyed it in a weird way. By the moaning sound, he knew that Elena was enjoying it better with all the pain. Then while he increased the speed of him fucking her, she started to fuck her pussy with that dildo so fast. He started to whip her a bit hard on her back. After a couple of times, it bled a lot, so he stopped. Now her entire back was covered in blood, but he didn't stop fucking her in the ass and she didn't stop fucking her own pussy with that huge dildo. Then she said, "Whip me harder daddy," but he knew that it would not be a good idea. So, he started to think about another way of inflicting pain. He saw the rest of the whiskey bottle and he managed to pick it up while his dick was still inside her asshole. Then he removed the lid and poured half of it on her ass. She screamed and stopped everything. Then she laid down on the floor. Now she is on the floor and she is crying while the dildo was still inside her pussy. Sanjay started to panic because he knew that it was too much of a torture even for Elena. Then he said, "I'm sorry." Then she looked at him. Her face was covered in snot and tears. Her lipstick was all over her mouth and her eyeliner was all around her eyes. Then through all that pain, she laughed and said, "I want more."

It was a huge relief for him because he thought that maybe she would press charges on him for torture. But now he understood that she genuinely had no limits when it comes to pain. So, he grabbed that dildo that was still inside her pussy and inserted all of it inside her pussy. She moaned while he did that, but it was obvious that she was too tired because of all the pain. Then he started to fuck her pussy with that dildo so fast for a couple of seconds. Then after he realized that she is at the peak of ecstasy, he inserted his dick inside her asshole again and started to fuck her as fast as he could. He tried to cum, but he couldn't because he was still in shock after what happened. Then it looked like she was getting bored. So, he turned her around to doggy style position as before and took the whiskey bottle and poured the rest of it all over her back. She couldn't scream because she was too tired. But by the sound of her weak moan, he realized that she felt the pain. He realized that her legs were getting weak and she was going to fall. So, he grabbed her by her waist and held her while he fucked her. Then he fucked her as hard as he could and this time, he managed to cum in about a minute. He didn't pull out. He wanted to cum inside her asshole, so he did. Then she fell on the floor and he laid next to her on the floor. Both were tired to the fullest.

They didn't talk for about 10 minutes. They just laid there. After that, Elena said, "Wow. That was the best sex I had in a long time. I haven't come like that in years. Thank you for that."

Then Sanjay asked, "When did you come?" because he honestly thought that she was just enjoying pain as pleasure.

Then she said, "Well, I came first when you inserted the dildo with whiskey. Then I came again while you were fucking me in the ass. Then I had a huge orgasm when you poured that whiskey on my ass. By the way, that was some good on the spot thinking. I think that is going to be my new favorite thing. Then I came again when you poured whiskey on my back. And I came again while you were cumming. So yeah, I came a lot more than you."

Sanjay was so happy because that was exactly what he wanted. Then she asked to go to the bathroom. While she was in it, he cleaned up the place because it was full of blood and looked like a murder scene. Then she came out of the shower bare naked. She took a tube out of her surprise bag and asked him to rub it on all the scratches from the whipping. After that, Sanjay asked her for her number and she said, "Oh sweety, this is a one-time thing. We can't have this kind of sex all the time. And I can't have normal sex with you after having this kind of sex. So, you understand that this is the last time we are going to see each other, right?" He got sad but he understood what she meant by that. It would be awkward for them to have normal sex after what they did. Plus, she would not be physically capable to have sex like that all the time because she must have lost at least a pint of blood from the whipping.

Then she collected everything she brought and put all of them in her surprise bag. She asked for a glass of water. After that, she put her clothes back on. She kissed Sanjay in the cheek and called a taxi and went home. It was the first and the last time he saw Elena. He messaged her on Tinder a lot but she never replied. He knew that it was a once in a lifetime thing. But after all, that one time was more than enough for him to satisfy all of his sexual fetish desires until he died.

THE END

CPSIA information can be obtained
at www.ICGtesting.com
Printed in the USA
LVHW050229161120
671797LV00008B/365